True A Fairy Tale Retelling of Puss in Boots

The Crown and the Sceptre, Volume 3

Kristina J Jordan

Published by Kristina J Jordan, 2021.

TRUE A FAIRY TALE RETELLING OF PUSS IN BOOTS

First edition. August 11, 2021.

ISBN: 979-8201295424

Written by Kristina J Jordan.

Also by Kristina J Jordan

The Crown and the Sceptre
Free A Fairy Tale Retelling of Rapunzel
Strong - A Fairy Tale Retelling of the Princess and the Pea
True A Fairy Tale Retelling of Puss in Boots
Pretty - A fairy Tale Retelling of the Frog Prince
Loyal - A Fairy Tale Retelling of Red Riding Hood

A slight grey shadow flitted through towering stone gates; pausing, ears erect as a frustrated roar echoed through an empty courtyard. Another roar sounded; closer and louder. The cat darted off the road, waiting until he was certain danger had passed. He picked down the steep road, keeping in the shadows of the looming trees. A silent figure slipped from behind a gnarled pine tree.

"You've wandered far from home small friend." The figure said.

The cat hissed, arching his back. Proud of his excellent senses; he hated being startled.

"No need to fear, we share the same goal." The man said, glossy lengths of black hair catching in the breeze.

"I swore a solemn oath to my master to protect his secrets until Carabas enjoys safety." The cat answered, a pang of regret threading his voice, allies were useful, and instinct told him this man was trustworthy.

"No matter, I'm a seer. Come to my village tonight, you face a long journey, and if we are to escape this current threat, we must work together. We have plans to discuss."

CHAPTER 1

Liliana clutched her shabby cloak tight around her slender shoulders, bracing her spine, warding off a shiver. Her breath rose; white misty tendrils whipped away by chilly wind biting through threadbare material. Once a lovely rose pink, her cloak had long faded to a grimy shade of grey. People thronged, crowding, pushing, and cheering as Princess Celine and her new husband, Crown Prince Alex of Iasia, rode by accompanied by a grand procession. The Crown Prince and Princess Celine were travelling through the small village of Annecy, en route to the kingdom of Iasia. Princess Celine would leave Lovan, beginning a new life with Prince Alex in the Iasian capital, Florin.

Liliana cautiously edged to the front of the crowd, craning her neck, longing to get a glimpse of the royal couple. She caught her breath. Celine's, more beautiful than Liliana imagined, famed golden hair and startling blue eyes were framed by a luxurious fur cape. Liliana sighed wondering how it felt to be warm, well-fed, and have splendid, rich things at her disposal. It had been years since Liliana had been so fortunate. So long that Liliana barely remembered how it felt not to worry about her next meal or whether her worn shoes would hold until she could afford another pair.

An unexpected shove caught Liliana off guard. She stumbled, directly into the path of one of the prancing chargers. The horse reared, its flying hooves narrowly missing Liliana's head as she made a clumsy attempt to dive out of his path, landing in a puddle.

"Whoa, settle boy." The prancing horse, calmed by his master's soothing voice, stilled. Only the tossing head and rolling eyes betrayed the charger's nervousness. Liliana glanced up, heart stuttering as she gazed into the most startling green eyes she had ever seen.

"Excuse me. I'm so sorry." Liliana jolted to her senses, scrambling to her feet. She didn't recognise the stranger, but judging from his expensive clothes and casual confidence, he was important. Liliana couldn't afford to offend anyone. She hastily stepped back, casting her eyes down respectfully. Wet sticky mud from the puddle seeped through the back of her dress, gluing cold material to the back of her legs. She longed to pull it away but clenched her hands firmly by her side.

"Are you hurt?" The green-eyed man jumped off his horse, holding out a hand to Liliana. She breathed in, distracted by his clean fresh scent. Bergamot and a hint of sandalwood rose above the smell of mud, horse, and rotting market vegetables. Liliana was suddenly aware of her untidiness. Her hair was damp and tousled from working in the garden; and her hands, dirty and calloused with labour. Not to mention, the spreading patch of mud on her patched dress.

"Yes, fine, sir. Thank you," Liliana's voice was low, cheeks flaming with embarrassment. She shifted, the eyes of crowd boring into her, no doubt wondering why this *gentleman* was speaking to a nobody like herself.

"Good." The man squeezed her shoulder, flashing a lightening smile before swinging back on his horse and re-joining the procession.

"Lily—Do you know who he is?" Blanchette hissed, nudging Liliana with a sharp elbow.

"No. Who?" Liliana turned to Blanchette, bruised and dazed from the experience.

"*Prince Landry.* Of Iasia. You know—Prince Alex's younger brother. He's unattached, you know." Blanchette eyed the broad back of the retreating prince, a calculating expression dancing in her blue eyes.

"Oh." Liliana sighed, failing to understand what Prince Landry of Iasia had to do with a poor Lavonian commoner, but she was positive Blanchette was about to instruct her.

"This was your big chance and you missed it. You could have flirted with Prince Landry a little. I mean, your clothes are shabby, but you're still pretty. If it was me, I would've jumped at the chance." Blanchette tossed blonde curls over her shoulder, putting her button nose in the air.

"Well, it wasn't intentional to go sprawling in front of his horse. Besides—he's a *prince*."

"That didn't stop Lucie. If she can marry a prince, we can get princes too." Blanchette wrinkled her nose distastefully. She had always been jealous of sweet, pretty Lucie, but now Lucie was married to Prince Frederich; Blanchette didn't have many opportunities to voice her negative opinions concerning Lucie. Not in public. Lucie was too popular.

"I'll remember that next time." Liliana's voice was dry, knowing full well she would never meet Prince Landry again. Humiliating herself in front of visiting royalty was hardly something Liliana planned to make a habit of.

Blanchette sniffed again, missing Liliana's sarcasm. Liliana rolled her eyes. Liliana and Lucie were best friends growing up, but that had spoiled. She had spoiled it, Liliana admitted. When Lucie's father lost his business— taking Liliana's father down with him— Liliana was bitterly angry, taking her frustration and anger out on Lucie. Something Liliana deeply regretted.

Blanchette, always competitive with Lucie, was quick to insert herself into Liliana's good graces. But friendship with highly strung, demanding Blanchette was very different than a friendship with Lucie who was always kind and loyal to a fault. Liliana desperately wished she could repair the relationship with Lucie, but Lucie was out of reach, leading the luxurious life of a princess in the Lovanian capital, Corvan.

"We should get to work. The tavern will be packed with all the crowds gathering to see Princess Celine off." Liliana ignored Blanchette's jibe and turned toward the Orc's Head— the tavern owned by Henri, Blanchette's father. Pouting, Blanchette reluctantly trailed behind her.

The door to the tavern swung open, letting out a blast of heated air mingling with the scent of frying onions, yeasty mead, and the meat stew Henri was serving tonight. Liliana hugged her arms around her stomach as it grumbled at the warm delicious smells. She would never admit it to Blanchette, but she was hungry. Lunch was meager; soup and a thin slice of bread. No butter. Since father became ill, she saved him the biggest portion— hoping, praying to nurse him out of the worsening illness that nagged him.

"Go to the kitchen and get started. We're busy tonight, girls." Henri bustled by, lugging a stack of wooden chairs. Extra chairs meant a late night. Liliana glanced across the packed room. Farmers lined the wooden tables, shoulder to shoulder with merchants and travellers, all joyfully celebrating the Princess's marriage.

Liliana quickly took an apron from a peg behind the kitchen door, wrapping it around herself. Henri was generous on busy nights and would send Liliana home with a packet of food, which if used carefully, could last Liliana and her father a few days. It was a good thing too; Liliana's cupboards were bare. Liliana quickly busied herself refilling drinks and ladling out big bowls of thick savoury stew simmering in the iron pot over the tavern's kitchen range.

The Orc's Head was almost busy enough for Liliana to forget her sore feet and empty stomach. At the end of the night, as expected, Henri handed Liliana a loaf of bread, still crusty and warm and a wrapped package of sliced meat and cheese.

"Well done tonight. Appreciate it." Henri patted Liliana awkwardly on the back as she slipped out the door toward home.

Liliana tore a chunk of bread, stuffing it in her mouth as she walked the cobblestone street toward home. Most townspeople were tucked in bed; life started early in the country; the square was deserted and silent. Liliana previously lived in a grand three-story house in the middle of Annecy, but circumstances since forced them into a tiny cottage at the edge of the village—a cottage inherited from her grandfather, the town miller. Milling was a trade he attempted to pass on to Liliana's father, who instead decided to go into business opening a prosperous mercantile on Market Square.

Liliana's father, Michel, had a thriving trade, until bandits destroyed the caravan routes run by Pierre, Lucie's father, forcing Michel and Liliana's family out of business. Liliana still winced and averted her eyes when she passed their old mercantile, now bought over by the bootmaker who managed to keep a thriving trade.

Liliana's brother, Gavin, constantly talked about reopening the mill, but it would require significant investment; investment Gavin didn't have. The wheel desperately needed repair after years of neglect.

The cottage door creaked as Liliana inched it open. Since father's health had taken a turn for the worse, he spent most of his day sleeping in the big chair by the fire. Tiptoeing across the room, Liliana tucked a blanket around his knees. Michel snorted, mumbling then settled in his chair peacefully. A snore escaped Michel's lips, as he turned his head to the side. Liliana decided not to wake him, so she added a few sticks of wood to the fire, grateful Gavin had stopped by earlier and filled the woodbox.

The crackling firelight flickered across Michel's face and Liliana noticed again the sunken cheeks and the shadows under his eyes. They seemed to grow darker every day. Ardus, the big grey cat, purred around Liliana's ankles as if sensing her distress.

"Hello, Ardus." Liliana stroked his soft fur, taking comfort in the loud rumble under her fingertips. Scooping up the cat, she headed for the tiny bedroom. It was a far cry from the pink carpeted room with its grand carved bed from her previous home—that had been sold when her father lost the mercantile. But it did the job. Shedding her dress, Liliana shivered into her thin nightgown and jumped in the bed, drawing the covers until only her nose poked from underneath the quilt. Ardus crept in next to her and the warm, vibrating body snuggled against her.

"What should I do Ardus?" Liliana whispered to the cat. She desperately wished Althea, the town herbwoman still worked in Annecy, but the healer was long gone. Althea moved to the castle soon after Lucie made her home there, taking a position of leadership in the mage guild.

In spite of a multitude of worries, Liliana's exhaustion soon lulled her into a deep sleep, the big green eyes of the cat watching her restless dreams.

CHAPTER 2

"Gavin. How did you get away so soon?" Liliana rubbed the small of her back; weeding vegetables was hard work. She had a streak of dirt across her face and her hair was askew.

Gavin threw his sister a wide smile. "Jon Pierre let me come for an hour to tell you my news."

"News?" Liliana picked up her basket, heading to the cottage. This sounded like the perfect opportunity for a cup of tea. Stopping at the well to splash water over her grimy hands, Liliana led Gavin to the kitchen.

"Tea, Papa?" Liliana asked Michel, pushing the dented kettle over the fire to boil. Liliana added precious tea leaves to each cup before slicing the fruit loaf that Henri had slipped into her package last night.

"Sorry, I don't have butter. Nana's not producing milk at the moment," she apologized to Gavin as he sat at the rickety table. "Now, tell us your news."

"Well...." Gavin drew out the moment, a grin splitting his face. "You know Jon is getting older." Jon, a local farmer had taken Gavin on to help with more arduous jobs on his farm.

"Yeesss." Liliana hovered impatiently, wondering what this had to do with Gavin's exciting news. Everyone knew Jon was elderly and getting frail. Jon always talked about selling his farm and moving south to the seaside fishing town he had grown up in. But Jon had been complaining and muttering about his aches and pains for years; no one actually thought he would sell.

"Jon sold the farm. Someone made him an offer and he accepted." Gavin paused dramatically.

"What?" water sloshed as Liliana nearly dropped the heavy kettle. "But what about your job?" There were few jobs available in Annecy, and Liliana wondered how she'd manage without Gavin if he moved. She bit her lip, waiting anxiously for him to continue.

"Wait, that's not all. You know how Jon lives on his own and never had children? He decided he wanted to make an investment. In me. In the mill."

"The Mill? Our mill?" Liliana plonked the kettle down, nearly missing the trivet.

"Yes, *our* mill." Gavin's grin grew wider. "So we can finally fix the mill the way we always planned to."

Liliana smiled back, Gavin's happiness was too contagious not to.

"And, I have other news." Gavin's smile stretched even wider.

"Well. What is it?" Liliana held her breath, wondering what could be more riveting than the news Gavin had just shared.

"I'm getting engaged." Gavin's eyes gleamed proudly, his chest puffed up.

"Oh. I wasn't expecting that. Engaged to who?" Liliana hesitated. She hadn't realized Gavin was courting anyone, not since he and Helen had parted ways. Thank goodness for that.

Liliana had read in a book—when they had books—that Helen meant tender and delicate. In her opinion, a name never suited anyone so little. Helen, the farrier's daughter was the least tender and delicate person Liliana knew. Ever. Brash, abrasive, and extremely bossy, she persecuted Liliana, along with the other younger children, as a little girl. Gavin insisted Helen changed her ways when he started bringing her around a few years ago, but in Liliana's opinion, Helen had only gotten clever at covering her domineering ways with a brittle veneer of politeness.

In spite of this, Gavin was desperately in love with Helen, and broken-hearted when Helen deserted him shortly after the collapse of Michel's business—another reason Liliana found to dislike the girl. She hoped this new love of Gavin's was more pleasant.

"To Helen." Gavin put his elbows on the table, shovelling in a slice of fruit loaf into his mouth. "I went straight over after I got the news from Jon. I can support a family now. And Helen never did court anyone after me." He gulped from his mug of tea.

Probably no one would have her, Liliana thought privately. For Gavin's sake, Liliana pasted a smile on her face. People could and did change; maybe Helen had changed too. Gavin lost more than Liliana when Michel's business failed; he'd planned to take over the mercantile, affecting him so severely that it was only recently that Gavin had gotten the bounce back in his step. Liliana badly wanted her brother to be happy.

"I'm sure you'll be happy together," Liliana spoke the truth here. Helen made Gavin happy. Gavin was the best brother; he deserved all the happiness in her opinion. She just wished it was with someone not quite so...difficult.

It was evening before Father woke so Gavin could tell him the news. Michel smiled weakly, content in the knowledge his son was happy and taken care of, but he fell asleep soon after, face grey in the late afternoon light.

"Is Father getting much worse?" Gavin hovered in the doorway, preparing to return to the farm. He wouldn't be back for days; he had to ready Jon's farm for the next owner.

"He is," Liliana answered, worry lurking behind her eyes. The fear Father's illness was serious and unrecoverable, encroached constantly on Liliana's thoughts. A heavy weight pressed constantly against her chest.

"He sleeps most of the time and barely eats. We've no healer or herbwoman now that Althea's moved; and I'm working nights, so father's alone in the evenings. I don't know what to do." Liliana glanced over her shoulder, making sure Michel wasn't listening. He lay asleep in his chair, mouth open, face slack.

Gavin squeezed Liliana's shoulder sympathetically. "I'll move home soon, and it won't be long until Helen joins us. Together, we'll nurse him back to health. Just hold on a little while longer." Liliana nodded, watching as Gavin disappeared down the path.

Unfortunately, Michel didn't have a little while longer. Over the next few days, Liliana's father worsened, getting weaker and weaker. Liliana had no choice but to ask Henri for a few days off to nurse him, assuring him she would be back as soon as she could. Henri instantly agreed, kindly sending Liliana home with a tureen of soup. That night, Gavin joined Liliana; the two took turns sitting Michel up, attempting to coax mouthfuls of soup into him.

As they sat, one on either side, holding their father's hand, Michel managed to speak one final time.

"I've left you a letter. It's in the box by the window. I want you to read it after I'm gone." Liliana had to lean close; Michel's croaking voice was so raspy and weak.

"Of course, Father. Anything," Liliana reassured him, stroking his withered hand. She attempted a watery smile, but her heart was cold. Father was still young, too young to leave her and Gavin. She willed back the tears that clogged her throat and pricked her eyes.

"I just wish I could do more for you." Michel's face was pale with the effort of speaking; he collapsed back on the bed, a sheen of sweat covering his brow. A few moments later, he was gone. His last breath leaving the room like a sigh.

Gavin gently set Michel's hand on his chest and took a deep breath.

"It's over." He looked at his sister, pain in his eyes.

I'm an orphan, Liliana thought numbness creeping through her body.

Liliana had been so young when her mother passed away. Only snatches of those memories remained—a wooden coffin covered with flowers; a silent house, echoing with the ache of loss. Father, sitting by the fire every night, lost in memories, oblivious to the needs of his young children. It wasn't until after—when Lucie and her sisters moved in next door that colour slowly returned to Liliana's world.

"I'll get the priest," Gavin's voice was wooden. Moving slowly, so slowly, he put on his coat and shoved his hat over his head. The door shut quietly behind him.

This was Liliana's first time alone in the tiny house. The darkness closed in around her, alive in its thick presence. The door creaked, and Liliana jumped, her heart in her throat, but it was the cat, who gracefully padded over and settled in Liliana's lap; a rusty purr rumbled deep in his little chest.

"I'm glad you're here, so I don't have to be all alone." Liliana stroked Ardus, soaking in the small comfort. The cat turned to look at her, a wise expression shining from his bright green eyes. A strange spark buzzed up Liliana's fingers, startling her with a tingling, almost stinging sensation.

"What was that?" Liliana jerked her hand away, looking at the cat suspiciously. "Did you do that?"

The cat didn't respond, merely staring at Liliana with unblinking eyes. "I'm imagining things," Liliana muttered. Shaking off the strange feeling still lingering, she put the kettle over the fire. The priest would arrive soon; she needed to prepare. At the window, a ray of light gleamed, reflecting off the metal lock on the wooden box. It would be much later before Liliana and Gavin remembered to open it and read the letter inside. The contents would change their lives forever.

CHAPTER 3

The door burst open, hinges protesting mightily at the rude treatment.

"I'm here." A loud, shrill voice announced. The overpowering scent of stale flower water assaulted Liliana's nose, making her sneeze.

Helen.

For the past few weeks, since the funeral, Helen was a constant, nagging presence at the little cottage. Liliana wondered what Helen wanted this time. Thankfully, Liliana was going to The Orc's Head soon. Liliana never thought she would be grateful for hours of backbreaking work, but anything that gave space from Helen was respite.

"I won't stay long." Helen's bright pink dress clashed with her curly red hair. Her cheeks were red with exertion; she flopped in a chair at the kitchen table.

"Do you have tea made? I'm parched," Helen demanded, ignoring the fact that Liliana was elbow deep in dishwater.

Liliana pressed her lips together as she silently moved the kettle to the hottest part of the fire and began measuring tea leaves into a mug.

"I just wanted to discuss our curtains." Helen took the cup Liliana offered without thanking her.

"You see, I thought blue material might match nicely with that rug." Helen gestured at the wool rug spread in front of the fire, one of the few luxuries they brought from the old house. It only escaped sale because of a stubborn stain. Liliana covered the stain with Michel's armchair. Even threadbare, the rug was still much too refined for the humble cottage dwelling.

"Yes. That sounds good," Liliana agreed politely. Helen had been unusually helpful and solicitous at Michel's funeral, organizing most of the affair. A godsend as Liliana and Gavin were too devastated to organize anything, but now, Helen never left the cottage, always asking incessant questions, always chattering, always full of opinions. Liliana's head spun from the constant effort of keeping up with Helen. Liliana longed to curl in a ball and be left alone to grieve.

"No, but what do you think, really? The blue? Or a nice bright yellow to pick out the design?" Helen's insistent gaze met Liliana's.

Liliana didn't care what colour the kitchen curtains were. Her head ached already. "The blue." Liliana pasted on a smile, making her voice as sure as possible.

"The blue? Are you sure? The yellow would be so cheerful." Helen cocked her head thoughtfully.

Liliana clamped her mouth together, wondering why Helen bothered asking if she had already decided.

"I think I might choose the yellow." Helen smiled beatifically.

"Sure, sounds lovely." Liliana held on to what she hoped was a gracious smile.

"I'm really sorry, I can't stay long. I have to get to work." Liliana untied her apron, smoothing her hair back.

"Oh yes, you're still at Henri's tavern. I don't know how you can take it. All those drunks." Helen shot Liliana an overly sympathetic look, followed by a smug smile. She never had to work.

"Well, I have to do something," Liliana pushed out the words.

"Well, you'll work here when the mill is operational." Helen smiled at her.

"Oh, yes, that will be nice." Liliana tried not to visibly recoil at the thought of spending every minute of the foreseeable future with Helen yammering in her ear. The questions, the sly digs, the constant chatter.

"Oh, another thing I came for," a satisfied smile settled on Helen's face. "We've set a date. Gavin and I."

"Oh, wonderful." Liliana jerked her head up; her strained smile slipped.

"Yes, I know it's soon, but Gavin and I can't wait to get settled; we're getting married as soon as the mill is up and running. A fortnight from now. We talked to the priest this morning." Helen smirked triumphantly.

A fortnight. Liliana's head reeled. Even in the countryside, a fortnight was a quick engagement. Unusually quick. She slid Helen a suspicious glance.

"Yes, we'll be sisters, like old times. I can't wait to spread the news, but of course I thought Gavin's family should know first, personally." Helen's wide smile turned almost feral as she lifted the cup to her lips.

"Yes, sisters, I can't wait," Liliana answered weakly. She firmly reminded herself that she and Helen were no longer children. She had grown up. So had Helen. Surely, Helen would behave civilly.

"I've had a lovely dress made for you to wear to the wedding. Beautiful. Come over tomorrow and I'll show you." Helen smirked again, setting her cup down and swanning out; she let the door bang shut behind her.

"TWO WEEKS?" LILIANA kicked a sawn log, then gasped as a sharp pain stabbed her toe. She grabbed her foot, sinking onto the sawdust covered ground.

"I know it's sudden. But we courted for ages—before." Gavin wiped his brow with the grimy edge of his shirt, streaking dirt across his forehead. The moment Helen left, Liliana had stomped straight behind the cottage. She found Gavin repairing the old millwheel.

"A little sudden?" Liliana repeated, crossing her arms tightly in front of her chest, voice getting more high pitched. "We haven't even had time to mourn father. What were you thinking, Gavin? This is ridiculous timing."

Gavin stood strong. "What was I thinking? I'll tell you what I was thinking. I was thinking I'm tired of being alone; I was thinking you might be lonely and appreciate company. I was thinking Helen is the person I plan to spend my life with. Why wait longer?" Gavin's voice was thick with emotion.

Liliana's mouth snapped shut as she dropped her arms. Gavin was serious. He loved Helen and there was nothing Liliana could do about it. She would have to make the best of the situation and hope Helen changed.

"I'm sorry. It's just that everything's changing and I'm having a hard time keeping up." Her eyes softened as she took in Gavin's repentant look.

"I'm sorry too. I should have told you what Helen and I were planning. I guess I got caught up in the excitement. But you'll love having a sister. After all, isn't a sister what you've always wanted? You and Helen didn't get along in the past, but give Helen a chance." Gavin offered his sister a pleading look.

Liliana rolled her eyes. Not getting along was putting the situation mildly. "Oh, all right," she relented, brushing crumbs of sawdust off her skirt.

"Good, because Helen's family is having us for dinner tomorrow night."

"*Us* as in both of us?" Liliana's eyes widened. Helen's father gave Liliana the shivers.

"Of course. We're family now." Gavin tweaked a strand of Liliana's hair, leaning over to pick up his mallet.

Liliana managed to get through dinner with Helen's family, suffering the lecherous stares of Helen's father. They were so obvious, they teetered on the edge of leering. Helen was obviously on her best behaviour, solicitously making sure her guests got the best of everything as they sat around the big wooden farm table.

"Delicious, did you make all this, Helen?" Gavin shovelled another bite of creamy, buttery mashed potatoes in his mouth.

"Of course." Helen made a show of pouring extra gravy on Gavin's plate. "It took me all afternoon to cook this dinner."

Liliana jerked her head up in surprise as Helen answered her gaze with a sharp look. She had seen Helen strolling through Market Square giggling with her friends earlier that afternoon; Helen wasn't in a hurry to rush home and slave over a hot stove then.

"Wonderful, really fantastic." Gavin's expression was full of admiration as he scraped the last bit of gravy-soaked food from his plate.

"Make sure you save room for pie; I've got some apple.... I mean blueberry." Helen quickly corrected herself at a subtle shake of her mother's head. "It's delicious with fresh cream."

"Oh yes, please." Gavin was used to eating bachelor food at Jon's farm. Not that Liliana was an awful cook, but she had to gather ingredients from what she scrounged from the garden and tiny wage at Henri's tavern. Anything would taste delicious after that meagre fare.

"I'm so glad you like it." Helen pushed back her mass of frizzy orange hair, simpering at Gavin.

"How is progress coming on the mill, young man?" Helen's father, Angun, a big burly farmer, took a break from ogling Liliana, pushing his plate aside and steepling his fingers in front of him.

"It's going marvelously." Gavin smiled proudly. "The mill will be completely operational before our wedding. We'll have some minor jobs after—tidying up—building some extra bins, the roof needs new shingles. But we can start getting an income. I have clients lined up already."

"Good. Good." Helen's father nodded. "I like hearing my Helen will be well taken care of." He smiled fondly at his only daughter.

"Yes, you'll be busy the next few months. But with our Helen helping, you'll be working smoothly in no time. Helen's a wonder with business. I've never seen our farm so prosperous as when Helen took over the trade aspect." Helen's mother, Floris, shot her daughter a proud look.

"And of course, a pretty thing like you, you'll be wanting to marry soon. You must have your fair share of suitors." Floris beamed at Liliana.

Liliana stared at the tablecloth, concentrating on the red stripe that ran down the centre of the pattern. Her cheeks flamed with embarrassment, heart thudding in her ears. She hadn't expected to be quizzed on her private life. Angun pinned his gaze on Liliana, openly admiring her.

"Liliana's been busy caring for father, she hasn't time for suitors." Gavin laid a comforting hand on Liliana's shoulder.

"Oh, of course. But now, you'll be able to marry someone. After all, you're not getting any younger." Flores gave Liliana an appraising look, and Liliana squirmed under its intensity.

"Oh, how about Darvyn? He's not married yet." Helen shot Liliana a sly grin as she spoke the name. They well knew Darvyn among the Annecy girls for being unpleasantly free with his hands. Liliana and Blanchette avoided him at all cost.

"Well, Darvyn's not said anything yet," Liliana answered politely. She didn't want to spoil Gavin's special night with awkward comments. She picked up her mag of cider, taking a long sip, avoiding Helen's sharp eyes.

"Well, I'm sure you'll be snapped up in no time," Flores spoke kindly. She sliced the pie and slid it onto the plates; berry juice bled through the flaky crust, puddling on the plates.

The delicious dessert distracted them from the strained conversation, allowing the rest of the evening to pass pleasantly enough. Most of the conversation was taken over by Helen's father and three older brothers enthusiastically discussing the fine details of Gavin's new business venture. It was increasingly clear to Liliana they intended for Helen to become a central fixture in the business, leaving Liliana on the fringe and preferably married to someone suitably far away. Gavin, so delighted to be included in this big boisterous family, didn't even seem to notice.

"You're quiet." Gavin nudged Liliana. They were on their way home. The moon had slid behind a patch of clouds and their way was only lit by the lamp that Gavin carried, casting its golden glow on the cobblestone street.

"Just a lot to think about," Liliana stayed carefully vague, not wanting to spoil Gavin's excitement about his new life. A life that increasingly excluded Liliana.

"Don't worry, sis, you know I'll always take care of you." Gavin read Liliana's thoughts, and Liliana took some small comfort because Gavin would always be her brother. No one could take that away.

CHAPTER 4

Gavin and Helen's wedding day arrived in a rush of activity. Liliana stayed up late every night helping Helen and Flores bake the Davaos, tiny cakes sprinkled with sugar and spices that would be handed to all the guests. Helen had proudly presented her with Liliana's dress—a garish, ruffle covered monstrosity that should have belonged to a twelve-year-old. Flores oohed and ahhed over the dress, but Liliana presumed by the hesitant expression flitting through Flores's eyes that the dress was as hideous as she suspected. She shrugged off the discomfort she felt surrounded by the stiff waves of scratchy fabric. She might look ridiculous and be excruciatingly uncomfortable, but at least it wasn't *her* wedding. If this made Gavin happy, then Liliana was willing to suffer through.

Before Liliana knew it, Liliana and Gavin arrived at the small chapel in Annecy Market Square. Gavin, handsome in his black waistcoat and polished shoes, was pale, sweating with nerves. Liliana waited with Gavin at the door to the chapel until finally, an hour later than expected, the bride arrived—a flurry of satin and ruffles topped by tortured orange curls.

Gavin sighed with relief as Helen met him at the chapel door. Taking his offered arm, she sailed confidently into the chapel beside him, leaving Liliana and Helen's family to trail behind them.

A wedding in Annecy was a big event, the whole of Market Square filled with well-wishers. Encased in her scratchy ruffled monstrosity, Liliana busied herself handing out the Davaos, smiling and nodding her thanks to the guests for attending. Soon, instruments were produced;

the square overflowed with dancing and laughter. Even Liliana forgot her lingering sadness and discomfort and joined Blanchette, laughing and swinging from partner to partner.

Stopping to catch her breath by the refreshment table, Liliana helped herself to a cup of cider, brushing falling strands of hair out of her eyes.

"Having fun?" Helen sidled up, a curious smile sliding across her face.

"Yes, I am," Liliana relaxed, deciding to forget past animosities and give Helen a fresh opportunity for friendship.

"That's good. Enjoy it while you can," Helen smirked, then pretended to stumble against Liliana, sending cider spilling down the front of her dress. "Oops, I'm so sorry. Clumsy me." Helen fanned her lashes in a pretence of apology.

Liliana gritted her teeth, staring at the growing wet patch staining the front of her dress. Just when she had decided to try...

"What happened?" Blanchette found Liliana helplessly blotting the mess with a napkin.

"Helen," Liliana huffed. "She did it on purpose."

"Probably," Blanchette agreed. "Helen always did love torturing you. Come on, I'll help you clean up."

Liliana followed Blanchette to the tavern where she gave her a damp cloth to soak up the worst of the stain.

"Where did you get that dress anyway? It's hideous." Blanchette wrinkled her nose distastefully.

"Helen had the dressmaker sew it for me." Liliana gave the colorful fabric a rueful look. Even with clothes scarce, Liliana doubted this particular dress would get a second outing.

"I see." Blanchette cocked an eyebrow.

Liliana sighed. Blanchette had gotten—well—*nicer* since Henri had reprimanded her over her behaviour toward Lucie, but she could still be blunt at times.

"I don't know what I'll do about Helen. We're sharing the cottage; it's a disaster," Liliana confided in Blanchette. "I try to be nice and sisterly, but it's clearly not working." Liliana gestured unhappily to the front of her dress. "And she's going to *live* with me. In a tiny cottage."

"You'll just have to show Helen she can't push you around. That's what I would do," Blanchette advised.

It was fine for Blanchette to take a stand. Her future as the pampered only daughter of a wealthy tavern owner was secured. But even with Gavin's support, Liliana realized her future was on shaky ground. Helen was making it clear that she wasn't welcome.

"How?" She raised her eyes to Blanchette.

"Easy, just give back what she's dishing out. That's what bullies understand." Blanchette swung her legs back and forth from her stool at the bar. Everyone was at the wedding; the tavern was empty. "If you let Helen push you around now, she'll never stop."

Liliana paused, giving the idea some thought.

"All right." She pressed her lips together as she made up her mind. "Let's do it."

CHAPTER 5

Liliana wiped her brow as steam rose up from a pot of potatoes. As she suspected, Helen did not cook the family dinner the night her and Gavin had gone to her house. In fact, Helen did not cook at all. And she made it clear that she didn't intend to learn any time soon. At least her father had sent along some livestock as a wedding present. They were housed in the shed behind the house. It was lovely having fresh butter, eggs, and milk, but really, all the extra work fell to Liliana as Helen protested she was far too busy helping Gavin with the milling business to do menial chores.

Although Liliana had never milked a cow or churned butter before, she learned quickly, adding these chores to the rhythm of her day. The cat, who had stuck to Liliana like glue in the past few days followed along, sitting by her side as she milked the cow and patting her knee occasionally if she forgot to give him his share.

"Is dinner ready yet? I'm starving." Helen threw herself into a chair at the kitchen table.

"Almost." Liliana turned the sausages in the pan. Although the mill was busy, no housekeeping money had appeared from it so, not wanting to meddle, Liliana took from her own small wages to supplement what came out of the garden. This afternoon, she had stopped at the butchers that afternoon to get the sausages for dinner.

"Where's Gavin?" she asked as she poured the carrots into the strainer.

"Oh, he had to finish up a few things at the mill." Helen tossed her hair over her shoulder. "I couldn't wait for him anymore, so I came on back to the house. What's that you're making? Sausages again?" Helen wrinkled her nose.

Liliana struggled not to roll her eyes. Sausages were the cheapest item at the butcher's and on the rare occasions they did have meat, featured heavily on the menu.

"Well, I'll be in our room; tell me when everything's ready." Without offering to help, Helen stood up abruptly and flounced to the small room she shared with Gavin.

"What are we going to do?" she addressed the question to Ardus who was winding himself around her ankles. Liliana had planned to start saving her wages, but feeding three people, one who was very picky, had made quite a dent in her savings. She would just have to speak to Gavin about pitching in. After all, the mill must be making a profit by now. A steady stream of customers had been in and out since they had opened for business.

Liliana pinched off a bit of sausage and gave it to Ardus who delicately lapped it from her hand.

"Is dinner ready?" Gavin stomped the dirt off his boots before entering the small kitchen.

"Yes. I'll just get Helen now." Liliana sprinkled a bit of salt over the potatoes and set the bowl in the middle of the table. "You look tired; is everything all right?" she paused at the door, looking at Gavin's face closely.

Gavin rubbed his hands over his forehead. "Yes. It's just a few teething problems. Nothing you need to worry your pretty head about." His voice was light, but the shadows in his eyes told Liliana he was worried.

"What teething problems?" deciding Helen could wait a minute, she sat down and waited for Gavin to explain.

"It's nothing really, just some cogs that need replacing. It's not grinding fine enough."

Liliana tried not to look worried. "How do we do that?"

"We'll have to get the smithy in."

Liliana knew this meant money. A lot more money. "Does Helen know?"

"She knows." Gavin's tight-lipped answer told Liliana there was more to the story than he was letting on.

"Oh, good, you're here." Helen sat at the table, taking the filled plate; without waiting for the others, she poured the gravy over the food, and began eating.

Liliana quickly offered Gavin the next plate, and he took the gravy pitcher, shaking out the last few drops over his own food.

"Who came in today?" Liliana attempted to clear the sour mood in the air by starting a cheerful conversation.

"Do you remember Marco, one of Henri's nephews? He bought a farm a mile out of town and he was there. Has two children now."

"Really? The last time I saw him, he was running around catching frogs. I can't imagine him being a father of two," Liliana's voice was high pitched with forced excitement.

"Yes, he was asking about father. He remembered him."

Liliana's smile slipped momentarily. She and Gavin had not talked much about the loss of their father, instead preferring to throw themselves into planning the wedding and starting up the mill again.

"I'm glad he has such good memories of him." She concentrated on scooping a bit of mashed potato onto her fork.

"He asked about you too."

"He did?" Liliana sawed off a tiny bit of carrot. She wondered what Marco would possibly want to know about her.

"Yes, his brother bought the farm next to his. Apparently, he's not married yet."

Liliana whipped her head up. "Do you mean Caelem?"

Helen looked up from her gravy-soaked meal to listen, a calculating glint in her eye.

"Yes. That's the one." Gavin leaned back in his chair.

"But he was a bully. Do remember how he treated that poor horse of his? The creature had to be put down." Liliana was horrified that Gavin would entertain the idea.

"But he was young then. I'm sure he's changed now. His brother was very nice today."

"You should at least give it a chance," Helen pitched in, voice sweet and honeyed. "After all, you can't be too picky anymore now that you're practically a pauper."

Gavin gave his wife a warning glance and she quickly dropped her eyes.

Liliana pushed her plate away. "No. I'd rather be alone than with someone like that. No one changes that much."

"But surely you didn't think you were going to stay here forever?" Helen ignored Gavin's glare.

"No, but I—" Liliana was dumbfounded. She knew she would have to move on at some point, but she never expected she would be turfed from her own home.

"I mean, who doesn't this house belong to anyways?" Relentless, Helen continued, her voice sending tendrils of doubt and panic through Liliana.

"Gavin?" Liliana turned to her brother.

"I don't know," Gavin answered slowly. "He left a letter. I suppose we could read it. But regardless of what it says, this is Liliana's home and she'll always be welcome here." He leaned back in his chair and crossed his arms in front of his chest.

Liliana shot her brother a relieved look.

"A letter? Where?" Helen's eyes searched the room as if expecting it to appear out of thin air.

Liliana knew she would get no peace until the letter was read, so she went over to the metal embossed chest that stood under the window. Fitting a small key into the lock, she turned it. The lid slowly opened with a large creak resonating through the small room.

The chest was one of the things Father had brought from the old house. It contained old business papers, no longer needed now, but he couldn't bear to part with them either. On top of a dusty ledger sat a folded sheet of parchment with Liliana and Gavin's name on it.

Throat tight, Liliana reached for the letter. This was her father's last wish and she wanted to hold the moment close.

CHAPTER 6

"Well?" Helen was nearly bouncing in her seat.

Slowly, slowly, Liliana opened the letter. Gavin leaned over her shoulder and they read together.

My dear children, I have lost most of my earthly possessions and my health is failing. I know I don't have much longer to live in this world. I wish so much I could give you everything, but alas, circumstances have changed. But what I do have is yours with all my blessing.

To Gavin, my firstborn son, I leave the mill and the house. It's not what it once was, but I have taught you everything you know to make it a great success. I wish you all the best.

To Liliana, my heart and my precious daughter, I leave my pocket watch and Angus, the cat. I trust I have taught you everything you need to make your life a great success. I wish you all the best.

With all the love in the world.
Father.

Liliana heard a choking sound and turned around to see Helen, face red from holding back a laugh. She held a hand up.

"I'm sorry, but a *cat*?" her face was contrite, but her voice still held a hint of merriment.

Liliana fought back the sting in her eyes and Gavin reached out and squeezed her shoulder. "It is a very nice pocket watch." He lifted the watch that had been tucked beneath the letter and handed it to Liliana.

Liliana took it out of his hand. The heavy silver watch had been her grandfather's. The sight of it brought back memories of being wrapped tightly in his arms, smelling the comforting scent of tobacco from the pipe he loved to smoke.

"It is a nice pocket watch." She twisted the chain around her fingers.

After work that night, Liliana lay in her bed, pressing a pillow tightly over her head. Gavin and Helen were arguing, their voices rising and falling in a steady rhythm. She cringed as she heard her name mentioned in a high-pitched voice. The arguments started the week after the wedding and gradually escalated in frequency and volume since. She squeezed her eyes shut, wishing she was somewhere else. *Anywhere* else really.

"At least you're here." She stroked Ardus who was lying next to her on the bed, tail curled neatly around his body.

"Of course, I'm here. I'm your cat, aren't I?" a matter of fact voice answered.

Liliana froze. She must be dreaming. She pinched her arm vigorously, sending a sharp pain shooting up her arm. No, she wasn't dreaming. She sat up, the pillow flying onto the floor next to the bed.

"What was that?" her voice sounded thin in the darkness.

"Me." Ardus stood and stretched his paws in front of him.

"But you're—a *cat*."

"Of course, I'm a cat." He proudly flicked his tail. "From the best family of cats too."

"But you're *talking*. Wait a minute, could you always talk?"

"Yes, but most people are so tedious, I really can't be bothered. But you're my mistress, so I'm making an exception."

Liliana lay back down. She would wake up in the morning and remember this as a strange dream she told herself as she closed her eyes and tried to breathe deeply.

"Awful even for a human, isn't she?" the cat continued calmly.

Liliana's eyes snapped open. The dream wasn't ending. "You mean Helen? Yes. She is awful; I don't know what he ever saw in her."

"I know." Ardus licked a paw daintily. "The *noise* since she's arrived. I can't sleep at all. She's scaring all the mice away too."

"I don't know what *I* can do about it." Liliana blew out a frustrated puff of air.

"Oh, there's always something you can do. You just need the gumption to do it."

"Like what?" Liliana was curious.

"Well, if a place is unpleasant, don't stay. That's what we cats do. How do you think I got here?"

"Oh. Where would I go?"

"Lots of places. The world is yours really."

"But, *how*. I don't have any money," Liliana's voice was sulky.

"Oh, you don't have to worry about that. Cat's don't have money and we're always just fine."

"But I'm not a cat."

"Well, if you're going to be fussy about it, I suppose we could arrange something. But with *me* to help, you don't really have to worry about all that."

Liliana was doubtful that a cat would be of that much help; it wasn't like she would be able to eat a mouse.

The tip of Ardus tail flicked. "Just go to sleep, little human; we can talk more about it tomorrow."

The voices on the other side of the wall were subsiding, and with the soothing purr of Ardus next to her, Liliana was finally able to fall asleep. When she woke up, Ardus was gone, a cooling spot next to her on the bed— the only sign that he had been there.

"Good morning." In spite of the strangeness of the night before, Liliana was feeling better this morning. She hummed softly as she broke eggs into the pan, stirring gently as they began to solidify.

"Good morning." Gavin's haggard face told the tale of a sleepless night. She slid the eggs onto the plate in front of him and began to butter the toast, topping it off with the berry jam she had made over the summer.

"Is Helen coming?" she asked courteously as she set a steaming mug of tea in front of him.

"No, she's not feeling well this morning." Gavin yawned as he dug his fork into the mound of scrambled eggs.

"Again?" a faint tendril of worry began to stir in Liliana's gut.

"Yes." Gavin didn't offer any more information. He ate steadily, keeping his eyes on his plate.

Liliana carefully worked the butter into the edges of her toast before taking a bite. It had been three, no—four months since the wedding, her mind worked overtime as she did the math in her head. And, Helen had been even more short tempered than usual, and was going to bed early and skipping breakfast....Her eyes met Gavin's over the breakfast table.

"Is Helen?"

"Yes. But she hasn't told her family yet, so we have to keep it quiet for now." His fork clinked against the plate as Gavin set it down.

Liliana remained silent at the table long after Gavin left. Finally, leaving the remainder of her toast sitting with the dirty breakfast dishes, she went out into the garden.

The garden was Liliana's thinking place. She loved putting things in the ground and watching them grow, and she loved that she could be alone for hours without interruption. Helen had an aversion to anything that looked like hard work, so she rarely came out to the garden. And the fresh clean air and scent of green growing things cleared her head.

It was here that Ardus found her, pulling the weeds out from around a patch of parsnips.

"What did they ever do to you?" Ardus curled his tail around his furry body as he sat on a flat rock nearby.

"Nothing." Liliana savagely pulled up another weed and flung it onto her growing pile with such vigour that it sent a small spray of dirt skittering through the air.

"It doesn't look like nothing." Ardus shook a few crumbs of soil from his grey fur before settling back down. "Those carrots didn't do anything to you."

"They aren't carrots; they're parsnips." Liliana sat back on her heels.

"It's just, everything is going wrong." She wiped her forehead with the back of her wrist, putting a streak of dirt on her face.

"Oh, is this because Gavin told you that Helen's pregnant?" the cat's voice was matter of fact.

"Yes," Liliana admitted. "It's just, I really don't think there's a place for me here anymore. But I don't know where my place even *is*."

Ardus began to smooth his already clean whiskers with his paw. "My offer still stands, you know."

"Thank you, but I don't know if I can just sail off into the sunset with nothing."

"You wouldn't have nothing," Ardus's voice was silky. "You would have *me*."

Liliana appreciated the offer, but desperate as she was, she had doubts that even a resourceful cat would be able to provide for a human's needs. She pulled up another weed.

"Let me think about it some more."

"Think about what?" a sharp voice behind her startled her as she tugged on a particularly stubborn weed, sending her sprawling backwards.

"Oh, nothing." Liliana stammered as she sat up and brushed off the dirt. "Just talking to myself."

Helen huffed and rolled her eyes. "Gavin said he told you our news."

"Yes, he did."

"Well, just make sure to keep it to yourself. It's better you find out now anyways; it will give you more time to find a new place to stay."

"New place to stay?"

"Well, the baby's going to need a room. And you saw the letter last night. The house is officially ours."

"Well, yes but I thought..." Liliana's voice trailed off.

"You thought what?" Helen's voice was scathing. "That you could just live off our charity forever?"

Liliana stood up, so shocked and angry, she didn't trust herself to speak.

Helen rubbed a hand proudly over her non-existent belly. "Let me know when you've found something so we can start getting the room ready." She turned and went back into the house.

Liliana turned back to the cat who had sat quietly on his rock watching the scene unfold. The only sign he had any opinions on the matter was the end of his tail, twitching back and forth.

"All right," Liliana addressed the small animal. "When do we start?"

Ardus sat up and stretched. "Well, we have to get ready first. I'm going to need a pair of boots. And a hat."

Liliana gave the little feline an incredulous looks. "Boots and a hat? What for?"

"I need them." The cat stretched languidly, flexing his toes in front of him.

CHAPTER 7

"Fine. I'll buy your boots and hat." Liliana huffed.

Liliana didn't know where one procured miniscule boots and hats, maybe doll's boots at the mercantile?

"A feathered hat?" Ardus demanded, patting Liliana's leg with an insistent paw.

Liliana rolled her eyes; holding in a smile. "A feathered hat."

"Good. We leave as soon as we get them." Ardus hopped off his rock and sauntered across the vegetables before leaping into the elderly oak tree at the edge of the garden.

When Liliana went inside, breakfast dishes were still strewn across the table. The only sign Helen had made an appearance was a cooling cup of tea and empty plate scattered with toast crumbs and streaks of congealed butter. Liliana muttered under her breath as she heated the kettle for the washing up.

Later, after scrubbing the kitchen, making lunch— a pot of bean soup Liliana left simmering at the back of the fire— and cleaning the little cottage until it sparkled, Liliana set off for town. She wrapped her few coins tightly in a handkerchief and pinned them in her pocket.

Liliana continued straight to the mercantile. It offered variety; there might be toys for sale. Liliana sneezed as she entered the small shop, the scent of dusty spices tickling her nose, itching the back of her throat. Liliana blinked, letting her eyes adjust to the dim light filtering through the shop window. Edging past the fancy lace and ribbons, Liliana headed to the back corner of the mercantile where a limited selection of toys lay on a wooden shelf.

"See anything you like?" Andre the mercantile owner, Michel's former employee, hovered behind the counter. He eyed Liliana speculatively; she didn't darken the doors to this establishment often.

"Just looking." Liliana lowered her head. There were three dolls. A floppy rag doll, with yarn hair and sewed on cloth shoes. A baby doll with dimpled bare feet made of china and a figurine with painted on shoes. Liliana's heart sank. Why was Ardus so awkward?

"Have you got any other dolls?" Liliana glanced around surreptitiously before asking the question. A single woman searching for dolls carried the potential for sending Annecy into a whirlwind of gossip. Fortunately, Andre didn't seem overly curious about the matter.

Andre scratched his whiskered chin thoughtfully. "I don't think so, but I'll check out back." Leaving Liliana alone in the shop, Andre disappeared behind the curtain leading into the mercantile's storage area. Liliana shifted from foot to foot, listening to the rustle of boxes and bags shuffling.

"Hello there," a voice startled Liliana. Eyes wide, Liliana whirled around. Close, too close, behind Liliana stood a strange man. Dark hair slicked back from a tanned face and large ropy forearms emerging from rolled-up sleeves told her he hailed from one of the farms clustered around Annecy.

"Hello?" Liliana hesitated. Although the man's face was vaguely familiar, Liliana couldn't place him.

"Caelem." The man grinned, displaying two rows of shiny white teeth.

"Liliana." She looked away, praying Andre would hurry.

"Your brother Gavin runs the new mill?" Caelem stepped forward, his large body crowding Liliana against bolts of fabric lining the back of the store.

"Gavin? Yes, yes, he does." In spite of the friendly smile, Caelem's cold eyes made Liliana's skin prickle. The bolts dug into her hip.

"I didn't know Gavin had such a pretty sister; I would have brought my grain in sooner." Caelem leaned forward, and Liliana cringed as his hot breath whispered across her cheek.

"Thank you." Liliana choked the words out, taking a tiny step sideways.

Andre emerged from the storage, brushing dusty hands together. "I didn't see any dolls. Should I order one?" he asked much too loudly for comfort.

"No, I'll manage." Liliana glimpsed Caelem's smirk out of the corner of her eye and desperately hoped he didn't plan to announce to the entire town she was looking for dolls. People would wonder why—that's how stories started.

"Dolls?" Caelem smirked. "Aren't you a little old to be playing with dolly's?"

"The doll is for a—friend." Not a lie, Liliana told herself. The cat was a friend—of sorts.

"Is there anything else you need, Liliana?" Andre asked politely.

"Yes, actually there is." Liliana fingered the bolts of fabric, settling on a rich chestnut felted wool.

"I'll take half a yard of this wool." Besides the material, Liliana chose a length of matching velvet ribbon and a plumy feather, its curling tendrils fading from luxurious chocolate brown all the way to light cream.

Liliana counted out the coins, carefully placing them in Andre's hand. Even though Caelem had wandered to the other end of the mercantile, pretending to peruse through seed bins, Liliana felt his piercing eyes fixed on her.

Liliana exhaled, tucking the wrapped package under her arm and left the mercantile, the bell chiming merrily behind her.

Slowly, Liliana strolled down toward Market Square, wondering where on earth she would find tiny shoes. The smell of sweet dough drew her steps toward the bakery; Liliana's mouth watered as she lingered in front of the large glass window, eyeing rows of iced cakes and sweet sticky rolls. The scent of sugar and cinnamon drifted in the air, so thick, Liliana could almost taste buttery sweetness melting on her tongue. Swallowing hard, Liliana hurried on to the shoemaker.

For Liliana, entering the shoemaker's shop was stepping back in time. It was the site of her father's old mercantile, the only difference outside was the hanging sign saying, "Aubercy's" in fancy gold script. Inside was an eerie reminder of happier times. The ancient wooden counter, bearing scars from years of use, even the same shelves, were now lined with stacks of leathers and shoe forms.

The bell tinkled, and the shoemaker appeared, brushing scraps of leather from his canvas apron.

"Hello, my dear, can I help you with anything?" Aubercy flicked his eyes toward Liliana's worn boots. She had brought them in to get resoled a few months ago. Even then, it had been obvious the boots wouldn't hold up much longer.

Embarrassed, Liliana slid her feet under the hem of her dress.

"No, I was actually wondering if you had baby shoes. Tiny ones. For a friend," she added hurriedly. Liliana's cheeks flamed at the curious glance the grizzled old shoemaker gave her. She desperately hoped he didn't think the baby shoes were for her.

"Not much call for baby shoes around Annecy." Aubercy scratched his head. This was true, shoes were expensive. Most babies wore thick wool bootie socks until they were walking age. Only wealthy people found it necessary to put leather shoes on babies.

"Oh." Liliana's head drooped.

"Hm... I'll look in here." The shoemaker rummaged through a cupboard full of lasts.

"Anna, Anna." He called to the back of the shop. Aubercy's wife, Anna, materialized, wiping floury hands on her apron.

"Do we have any baby shoes? Small ones. Liliana here wants to buy them for a friend," Aubercy explained.

Anna pursed her lips, drawing her brows together. "I think we did have a pair. Do you remember we made some to celebrate the birth of the prince? For the old shopfront window?"

A ray of hope kernelled in Liliana's chest. Maybe Aubercy did have tiny shoes. The prince was older than Liliana; they were bound to be ancient. Even so, shoes were shoes; they might be doable.

"Ah yes, that's right. Lovely little boots, beautiful coloured stitching around the sides. That was high fashion in those days. Now, where did we put them?" Aubercy continued to rummage, tossing out an assortment of tools and accoutrements until piles surrounded him on all sides.

"Ah ha. Here we are." Aubercy drew out a small wooden box and opened it proudly. Lying in a nest of faded blue linen, sat the tiniest pair of leather boots Liliana had ever seen.

"Oh, they're perfect." The words rushed out before Liliana could stop them.

Anna smiled, touching the miniscule boots delicately with her worn finger. "We made those boots when we first started the business. Called them our good luck charm. Funny, I'd almost forgotten them." Anna laughed, a soft smile crinkling the lines around her eyes.

"How—how much?" Liliana nervously fingered the remaining coins in her pocket. The shoes were so beautiful, so impeccably made, she wondered if she could afford them.

"Your father and I did a lot of business together in the past. And it's a shame all he suffered at the end—the illness. If you want them, I'll give you a deal; they're yours for two small silvers." Aubercy's kind eyes warmly regarded Liliana.

"Thank you," Liliana's voice was low as she stifled the flood of emotion. The loss of her father rose fresh; being in the place where they spent so much time together was bittersweet and searingly painful. Aubercy's kind gesture was almost too much for Liliana to bear.

"I'll wrap the boots for you." Seeing Liliana on the verge of tears, Anna came to rescue. She took the tiny boots, gently wrapping them in brown paper, tying it off with a length of red and white striped string.

"Here you go, dear." Anna handed the tidy package to Liliana, who bundled it under her cloak with the other before re-emerging into the bright sunlight.

CHAPTER 8

Late that night, when Gavin and Helen were sleeping soundly, Liliana got to work. Using a small bowl for a form, she shaped the felt material around it before pouring boiling water on it, leaving it to dry in the garden shed; safe from Helen's prying eyes.

Late the next evening, Liliana trimmed the felt, then carefully stitched on a flaring brim, finally attaching the curling feather to the velvet. Proud of her accomplishment, Liliana stood back admiring her efforts.

The hat was tiny, perfectly suited for the debonair little cat. Tucking the boots and the hat together behind the garden tools, Liliana left the shed, gently closing the door behind her.

"Why in Kings Forest are you skulking around our shed at midnight?" Helen's voice dripped with disdain. She stood in the cottage, her long white nightgown flapping around bare legs, orange hair askew with sleep.

"Nothing," Liliana kept her voice calm and flat. "I just couldn't sleep is all."

"I suppose now is the best time. We need to have a chat." Helen pulled up a chair.

"About what?" Liliana remained standing.

"About you, of course." Helen's voice was unnaturally pleasant, honeyed. "Caelem came to the mill today."

"Oh?" Liliana kept her answer short. Her heart plunged as she hoped this conversation didn't go the direction she thought. Liliana didn't know what her future held, but she certainly knew what it *didn't*. Caelem.

"Caelem wanted to speak to Gavin and ask for your hand." Helen's eyes gleamed.

"What did Gavin tell Caelem?" Liliana held her breath, waiting for an answer. Surely, Gavin had the sense to refuse Caelem.

"Gavin said he would have to speak to you first." Helen rolled her eyes at the ridiculous idea of letting Liliana make up her own mind. "Ahh... I know what you're thinking." Helen's voice was sensible. She folded her hands primly on the table. "But you need to see facts, Liliana. You don't have options. Facts is, Caelem's a good suitor. Caelem's got a farm. A *rich* farm. Did you really think you could aim higher?"

"What about the rumors?" Caelem was known for being violent and mean. Liliana shivered as she remembered his cold eyes scouring her from head to toe.

"Just rumors," Helen scoffed. "You know you can't go around believing everything you hear. Thing is, when the baby comes, we'll need the space. We can't build right at the minute. You know that. The blacksmith alone will bury us in debt."

"It will?" Liliana knew smithy's work was costly. But hadn't realized the situation was dire.

"Nothing we can't handle, of course.... eventually," Helen added hastily. "But we can't afford to keep you here anymore."

Liliana wondered resentfully who Helen thought was feeding her.

"What's Gavin's opinion on that?" Liliana forced her gaze straight ahead, keeping her face very, very still. "Oh, Gavin agrees with me, obviously," Helen's voice was airy. "He just doesn't know how to approach the subject. I mean, you're Gavin's sister; you know how he hates to hurt anyone's feelings."

Clearly, hurting people's feelings wasn't something Helen took issue with. Liliana felt numb.

"All right," Liliana's voice was even. Expressionless.

"All right, what?" Helen's eyes glittered, a hint of a smile crossing her lips.

"All right, I'll go." Liliana sighed woodenly.

"I'm glad we had this talk." Helen stood up from the table and brushed her hands down her wrinkled nightgown before returning to bed, a look of supreme satisfaction plastering her face.

Numbly, Liliana drifted to her tiny bedroom. Folding her clothes into a neat pile on the pinewood chair, she slid into her nightgown and got into the bed.

"I've seen foxes more friendly that that one," Ardus spoke from his seat on the windowsill. With one graceful leap, he landed, light as a feather, on the bed next to Liliana.

"I see you have my hat and boots ready." Ardus nudged Liliana with his nose until she began stroking his fur.

"Yes." Still stinging from the conversation with Helen, Liliana wasn't in the mood for chitchat.

"That's good. As soon as Gavin goes to the mill, we can leave."

"Just sneak off without telling anyone?" Liliana lifted her head.

"You heard what Helen said. It's time."

Liliana lay her head back down. She wasn't hurt that Helen didn't want her here, but hearing that Gavin agreed with her, that pierced her like a knife.

"All right," Liliana agreed; mingled terror and excitement creeped through her. "First thing in the morning."

CHAPTER 9

Keeping a secret from Gavin was hard. Excruciating.

Liliana guiltily bit her tongue over breakfast. It felt *sneaky* leaving her brother without saying goodbye. But Liliana knew if she told Gavin she planned to run who-knows-where with her cat—her talking cat — Gavin would convince her to stay.

With Caelem.

That wasn't an option.

Liliana watched Gavin leave for the mill, whistling jauntily. Then she sprang into action. Scooping up her pocket watch and a satchel of clothes—she didn't have much—Liliana tiptoed to the kitchen. Here, she gathered bread she'd baked the day before, dried meat, and packets of dried food. Liliana reasoned since she had bought the food, it was hers. Liliana placed a note inside her bedroom, then glanced around the cottage before closing the door gently behind her. She went to the shed for Ardus's boots and hat.

"Are you planning to wear these now?" Liliana asked Ardus, who was resting on an upturned metal bucket. She held up the tiny items.

"I don't need them just yet. Put them in your satchel. And you'll need string and a basket."

"Will that basket work?" Liliana pointed to the basket she used to carry vegetables to market.

"It will do."

Liliana obediently placed her satchel in the basket with the ball of string she used to tie up the beans. "Anything else?"

"We're ready. I'll meet you at the place where the willow tree grows over the bridge." Ardus jumped lightly to the windowsill, disappearing into the sunny garden.

Liliana carried the basket on her hip, attempting to look casual as she strolled through Market Square to the other side of Annecy. The market was beginning to open; venders busily were setting up their stalls.

"Liliana."

Liliana groaned. Blanchette.

Blanchette would insist on lingering for a chat. Nosy as always, she would ask why Liliana was heading the opposite direction from her cottage, buying nothing. Liliana turned, pasting a casual smile on her face, waiting for Blanchette to catch up.

"I heard your news; I can't believe you didn't tell me last night," Blanchette scolded, scampered to Liliana's side. As usual Blanchette had overdressed for market day, the giant cluster of colorful feathers on her hat was nearly the size of her head. The feather's wobbled and bobbed energetically in her excitement.

"What news?" Liliana frowned.

"You're getting married. That news, you big ninny."

"To who?" A feeling of dread crept up Liliana's spine.

"To Caelem. I have to say it shocked me when I heard. You know Caelem's a little..." Blanchette's voice trailed off uneasily. Blunt as she was, Blanchette didn't want to criticize her friend's fiancé.

"Oh, no, definitely not engaged," Liliana jumped in, horrified. She glanced around the busy market square, wondering how quickly this juicy news had spread.

"Well, Caelem came into Orc's Head late last night; you'd left. He rambled on and on about your engagement. Said he spoke to Gavin yesterday." Blanchette's concerned gaze met Liliana's.

Liliana shook her head vehemently. "Caelem did speak to Gavin. But it's my choice. I'm not getting engaged. Not yet, and definitely not to Caelem."

"Oh." Blanchette deflated, her feathered hat drooping, disappointed her chief topic of discussion was off limits.

"Let's look at fabric stalls. Father's giving me a new dress; I'm looking at colours," Blanchette cheered, cozily linking arms with Liliana.

Liliana glanced at her friend, regret etching her features. Blanchette had her flaws. Big ones. But she'd always stuck by Liliana's side. "I'm taking these parcels over the bridge." Liliana kept her words purposefully vague, hoping Blanchette would think she was making a delivery for the mill.

"Oh, I see." Disappointed, Blanchette released Liliana's arm and stepped back. Wishing she could say goodbye properly, Liliana reached out and gave Blanchette a hug, narrowly avoiding a jab in the eye from Blanchette's hat.

"What was that for?" Blanchette wrinkled her nose in confusion.

"You're a good friend." Liliana stepped back, blinking moisture from her eyes.

Blanchette giggled. "You're so silly sometimes. I'm off to the stalls. Catch up with you later?"

Liliana nodded quietly then continued on her way, turning once to look back at Blanchette's feathered hat bobbing and weaving through the crowd.

Ardus was waiting at the bridge, pacing as the tip of his tail twitching impatiently.

"Sorry I'm late," Liliana puffed, leaning against the stone wall at the side of the bridge. "I had to get away from Blanchette."

"No matter." The cat rubbed his head against Liliana's shoulder. "We aren't going too far today." Ardus hopped down, sauntering along the path.

CHAPTER 10

Hours later, Liliana was still walking.

They left the main road at noon, taking a rutted path that wound through the thickest part of the forest. Light filtered through trees that soared overhead in a canopy of green.

"Where are we going?" Liliana asked, plodding around a patch of sticky mud. They hadn't stopped for lunch, instead keeping a slow but steady pace, and Liliana was starving and very thirsty.

"You'll see," Ardus responded mysteriously. The little cat was untiring, small paws steadily eating up the miles as he stalked along, tail held proudly upright.

"Can't we eat stop for lunch?" Liliana complained. She was regretting bringing the basket. It was extremely awkward to carry; the handles had sharp edges that dug into her fingers, causing red welts.

"You humans, so particular about getting your meals like clockwork." The cat flicked his tail, ignoring the fact that he demanded a saucer of milk at exactly six every evening.

"Oh, thank goodness." Liliana spotted an overturned tree near the side of the path ahead. She sat down, flexing her hands. Red lines crisscrossed her fingers, mimicking the pattern of the basket. Rummaging inside, she pulled out the loaf and the dried meat, fashioning a sandwich. It was dry, but edible. For the cat, she picked out of the meat and set them on the log next to her. Ardus perched next to Liliana, tearing the meat into tiny pieces and nibbling daintily.

In no hurry to walk again, Liliana stretched her legs, observing her surroundings. Liliana had never ventured this far deep into the forest.

Her previous excursions were only on well-travelled roads to nearby towns or the capital city—Corvan. Even that had been rare.

The trees grew thick, light filtering dimly through the foliage; only a few dancing flecks of gold lett Liliana know the sun still shone high. Birds chattered and chirped in the trees overhead; occasional rustling told Liliana there were other creatures lurking as well. A squirrel scolded from a tall oak, shaking his tail before disappearing into a knothole.

"We'll have shelter tonight. Don't worry." Ardus read Liliana's thoughts. He carefully licked his whiskers and paws before leaping from his perch.

Before leaving, they paused at the trickling stream rushing through the ravine. Liliana drank deeply before carefully filling the leather waterskin she had brought with her, fastening the wooden lid carefully to make sure it wouldn't spill.

Darkness was creeping over the forest before the cat finally stopped. "Here."

Liliana looked around at the same packed dirt path they had travelled all afternoon.

"Follow me." The cat left the path, trotting through thick trees, leaving Liliana to blunder behind him. After ten minutes, they reached a wooden hut.

"We'll stay here tonight," Ardus announced. "The key is under that rock by the kitchen window."

Liliana set down her basket and went over to what she assumed was a kitchen window. Sure enough, under a heavy moss-covered rock was a big iron key. Liliana fitted it into the lock, and it slid open. Too grateful to question how Ardus knew about the mysterious accommodation, Liliana ventured inside. The cabin was surprisingly cozy; tidy row of dishes stacked the kitchen shelves and airtight cannisters of flour, sugar, tea, and other supplies lined the cupboards underneath. Across from the kitchen area was a bed covered with a colourful quilt. Matching cushions decorated the two chairs that sat on either side of the fireplace. A puff of dust rose from one of them when Liliana patted it. She sneezed.

"We'll be safe here." Ardus curled up on the large braided rug in front of the fireplace. "Just bolt the door before you sleep. And bring in enough wood to keep the fire until morning."

"Why, is it dangerous here?" Liliana knelt in front of the fireplace and began setting up the kindling.

"Wolves, but they stay outside at night." The cat yawned, laying his head on his front paws.

Liliana sat back on her heels, hairs rising on her neck. Annecy had been troubled with wolves years ago, but Liliana assumed the wolves had moved on. It was disconcerting to discover she had been unknowingly sharing the forest with them all day.

"Are there many wolves?" Liliana held the tinder to a curl of wood with a shaking hand, trying desperately to coax out a flame.

"Several. I think they're looking for something in particular. They shouldn't bother us." Ardus lay his head on his paws, seemingly unconcerned about the large carnivores lurking in the woods.

It took Liliana several tries to light the fire, but finally, a flickering light filled the room. Just in time, thick darkness had settled over the forest. Liliana spent the next ten nerve-wracking minutes rushing back and forth from the woodpile until she had enough wood stacked up to last until morning.

After a cold dinner of bread and meat, Liliana curled up on the bed, still fully dressed, and fell asleep until morning. Her last memory was of a small furry body snuggling against her and the rumbling purr that accompanied it.

CHAPTER 11

Liliana's eyes snapped open.

The crackling fire had faded to a pile of glowing embers. They did little to light the dark cabin. But it wasn't the darkness unsettling Liliana. She strained her ears.

In the distance, she heard something.

Howling.

Wolves.

Liliana froze, waiting, hoping it was an overactive imagination. Another howl; closer. Nudging Ardus gently aside, Liliana padded to the fire, adding logs before checking the doors and windows were securely latched.

Ignoring the dust, Liliana lay back in bed, pulling the quilt tight over her head, shivering even though the night was warm.

The wolves grew closer and closer. The howls shook the tiny cabin. For the first time, Liliana realized how alone and defenceless she was. What was she thinking following a cat into the depths of the forest?

Liliana lay awake the rest of the night, although Ardus snoozed on, unfazed by the chilling howls. The wolves were so close, Liliana wondered if they were right on top of her. One wolf even approached the door; sniffing and clacking razor-sharp claws against the wood. Liliana hoped desperately that the bolts would hold tight as she wished for morning.

Eventually, dawn arrived, announcing its presence with thin grey light. The wolves disappeared just before morning, but not before one final blood curdling chorus. Liliana peeked from under the quilt, grateful to be alive. Ardus was *still* sleeping, warm body pressed up against Liliana, the small chest rising and falling rhythmically. Edging away slowly so she wouldn't waken him, she crept to the kitchen. Liliana's bread and meat would only last another meal. Liliana needed more food. Again, Liliana questioned her impulsive decision to follow a cat to an unknown destination.

"Look behind the cannisters." Liliana turned her head. Ardus regarded her with bright, unblinking eyes.

Liliana pushed aside the cannisters. In the depths of the cupboard were hidden rows of jars. She drew one out. Preserved food. Some of them were filled with dried food, some pickled. Dried, salted meat, reasonably fresh travel cakes, and sacks of beans and lentils.

"Take whatever we need," Ardus encouraged her.

Liliana nodded. Taking a hanging satchel from the kitchen hook, she filled the satchel with food wrapped in cloths, replacing the jars neatly back in the cupboard.

"I'll get my own breakfast." Ardus hovered by the kitchen door until Liliana slid the bolt, then sashayed into the clearing. Liliana followed him hesitantly. Circling the cabin were giant paw prints, so big, Liliana could fit her foot right inside them.

"What *are* these creatures?" Liliana breathed, skin tingling.

"The wolves are newcomers to this forest," Ardus answered, sliding one of the prints with a passing glance. "Searching for something, judging by the howling. The wolves won't harm you if you keep out their way. But they certainly are curious about newcomers." Ardus was switching into hunting mode, ears flat against his head, slinking low across the ground.

Deciding to leave Ardus in peace, Liliana retired to the cabin, sliding the bolt firmly into place behind her. Just in case.

Ardus returned half an hour later, proudly dragging a large wood hen, laying it dutifully on the doorstep. Glad Gavin had taught her to clean poultry, Liliana soon had it in the pot with some carrots and an onion she found in the garden. While the stew bubbled, Liliana gave in to her curiosity about the cabin, opening every cupboard and closet. So many questions churned in her mind.

Who did the cabin belong to? Why so deep in the forest? Most of all, who were its mysterious owners? But there were no answers from Ardus, who clearly didn't care.

Ardus watched, amusement glinting from his green eyes as Liliana searched under the bed, sneezing at the dust bunnies crowding the dark corners.

"You won't find anything," Ardus told her, stretching languidly on his side by the fire.

This was the only answer Ardus would give her, and Liliana had to content herself, enjoying the shelter and food provided by the cabin.

"Make sure you have everything packed. We leave at first light in the morning," Ardus told her as Liliana tucked into her stew that night. She placed the rest carefully into a jar. It would do for lunch tomorrow.

"I wish we could thank them," Liliana murmured, scrubbing the pot and wiping it dry before hanging it back on its hook.

"We'll have our chance," the cat assured her, wiping his whiskers.

That night, the wolves arrived again. After listening to the howls rise and fall, Liliana finally fell asleep under the quilt.

"Wake up, sleepyhead." Ardus kneaded Liliana with his paws until she groaned sleepily, rolling over. The bed was so comfortable and warm.

"We have to leave." Ardus didn't stop until Liliana sat up, rubbing her tired eyes.

After a hasty breakfast of griddle cakes, Liliana took one last glance around the cabin, making sure everything was tidy before locking it, tucking the key under the mossy rock. Hefting the weighty bag of food slung over her shoulder, Liliana picked up her basket, bulky from the bedroll Ardus insisted she bring — apparently whoever owned the cabin wouldn't mind—and followed Ardus back to the forest path.

CHAPTER 12

Ardus was unusually brisk for such a small animal, strutting as if he owned the forest. In a way, he seemed to, Liliana mused. Again, they walked steadily. Here, the path widened; Liliana began to see signs of civilization. A cut tree, scattered ashes from a campfire, even a makeshift bridge spanning the rushing brook. Nothing more than a few logs nailed together. Still, Liliana was hopeful they would soon be nearer to other humans.

"We'll stay here tonight." The little cat veered off the path, stopping in a small clearing. This was no well-stocked cozy cabin; it was simply a flat area between three trees.

"What about the wolves?" Liliana shivered, remembering the size of the wolf prints.

"The wolves don't travel this far. As long as we build a substantial fire, we'll be safe."

Not willing to risk being at the mercy of giant carnivorous predators, Liliana spent the next hour gathering sticks. She built a roaring fire, even dragging a small log over and shoving it into the flames. Ardus watched, amusement glinting in his liquid green eyes, but said nothing.

Over the next few days, Liliana and Ardus walked steadily, keeping as far away from civilisation as possible. Ardus caught enough game to keep Liliana's store of supplies supplemented. The terrain changed as they travelled, the soaring canopy of trees giving way to sky overhead. Rocks and boulders, gleaming wetly with dew, dotted the rich dark soil.

There were hills too. The forest had been flat with fairly smooth paths to follow, but now Liliana and Ardus were climbing.

"This way." Ardus steered Liliana from the path, hastening their pace, moving from a saunter to a fast trot.

"What's happening?" It was an hour past midday, nowhere near time to make camp yet.

"Shh..." he demanded, tension evident in every line of his tiny body; Ardus crouched behind a leaning pile of boulders. "Get in there," his voice was a hoarse whisper.

Liliana squeezed between the crack in the boulders, wedging inside the pile. A thin crack between two boulders gave her a limited view of the path. She pressed her eye to the opening, spotting the reason for the cat's distress.

Riding down the path was a group of travellers, dressed in the distinctive woven pattern of Antarai, a fierce tribe originating from the western mountains of Iasia. Liliana wondered what brought Antarai so far east. It appeared they'd been travelling for some time. Their sturdy ponies sported jingling harnesses, bulging packs and saddlebags, colourful Antarai woven blankets peeked from underneath the saddles.

Liliana slowed her breath, trying to be quiet and still. Ardus was nowhere in sight, probably up a tree somewhere, thought Liliana, pressing her eye closer.

Liliana heard dogs before she saw them. Yapping and snarling, the lean rangy animals bounded together, clustered in the middle of the group. Liliana shrank inside her nook. The Antarai were renowned hunters, and their dogs were excellent trackers. One of the smaller dogs started it, a tan coloured male with brown markings on his back. He pricked up his pointy ears and ducking his head, snorting and barking.

"Manaan, what is it boy?" an accented voice shouted. The dog responded by lifting his nose, whimpering and prancing in excitement.

"Manaan's scented something," one of the men shouted. He flung his arm in the air, signalling, and the dogs got to work, sniffing, searching, barking. Liliana froze, wondering what her next move should be. She didn't look forward to meeting a group of strangers on the trail, but it appeared Liliana had no choice. The dogs had discovered her hiding place. Yipping proudly, the dogs surrounded Liliana's hiding place.

"Well, look here." A tanned face surrounded by shiny black hair peered into Liliana's crack between the largest rocks. Liliana's throat closed. Caught.

"What is it?" another face appeared, this man older, threads of grey tracing his black hair.

"It's a girl." The first man uttered a sharp command, and the dogs dispersed, returning to their cluster among the horses.

"A girl?" Liliana felt claustrophobic; her heart hammered against her chest. They surrounded her, bright inquisitive eyes regarding her with curiosity.

"What are you doing here alone?" One man glanced up the path to see if Liliana had companions.

Liliana's eyes darted frantically; the rumors about Antarai were rife with warnings about their violence and disregard for human life and property.

"I'm meeting someone further down the trail." Liliana hoped they would leave her alone rather than meet the wrath of her supposed travelling companion. Not the time to mention her travelling companion was a magical cat.

"Oh, so are we." Another man grinned, showing two rows of shiny white teeth.

"A pretty girl like you shouldn't be traveling alone." The older man moved back to let Liliana climb from her hiding place. His embroidered leather vest gaped open and Liliana's eyes popped as she spotted a large shiny knife tucked into his waistband.

"Would you stop scaring the poor girl?" Another face joined the crowd around Liliana. Liliana breathed a sigh of relief. This arrival was a woman. A beautiful woman. Dark hair braided around her head, and a colourful dress sewn with rows of tiny coins caught the light, glinting when she moved. The men moved back respectfully to let her pass.

"I'm Sokdi." The woman held out a hand, helping Liliana scramble over the rocks. "These big lumps are harmless."

Liliana stood, brushing dirt and leaves from her dress.

"We're headed to the capital. If you're going that direction, you're welcome to join us. He's right, you know; it's not a good idea to travel these roads alone." Sokdi smiled warmly.

Liliana wished Ardus was around to advise her, but the cat remained stubbornly out of sight. She would have to decide herself.

"All right," Liliana found herself agreeing. She was glad for the company, and something about Sokdi was warm and motherly. Liliana allowed Sokdi to lead her away.

Before she could blink, the Antarai put Liliana on a spare pony, placing her next to her protector, Sokdi— the only woman in the group. The band was comprised of fifteen Antarai. One man, Chodos, Sokdi's husband, added Liliana's basket to a packhorse, and they were off. Just like that. Liliana's head reeled with the speed and efficiency of it all. She hoped Ardus would follow her; once or twice, she glimpsed grey fur slipping through the trees beside her.

Liliana found the Antarai more than pleasant. The air filled with laughter, chatter, and even at times, song. She watched quietly from her pony beside Sokdi as the hours slipped by. Before she knew it, they stopped in a small clearing. A rushing brook provided cool, clear water. The ground was flat and dry, perfect for a campsite. Antarai set up camp swiftly, each person comfortable with their own task, and before she blinked twice, Liliana was sitting by a fire, surrounded by a neat circle of pitched tents. The ponies were each munching a bag of grain and the dogs basked contentedly near the fire. Lukdee would feed them later.

"Come," Sokdi smiled, beckoning. Liliana stood stiffly—she was unaccustomed to riding—and followed the older woman who had a canvas bag slung over her shoulder.

"We're going to bathe," Sokdi explained, leading Liliana upstream. They walked until they found pebbled banks; ahead, the rushing water fell over a large rock, forming a deep pool. It was green topped with foamy white.

"Here, use this." Sokdi handed Liliana a large cotton cloth stitched to form a loop. Liliana stared at the cloth, confused.

"Like this." Sokdi laughed. She stepped gracefully inside the circle and drew the cloth across her chest, folding it tight until it fell to her knees, then deftly removed her clothes underneath.

Liliana nodded in understanding. This must be how Antarai women protected their modesty while bathing in rivers. She clumsily folded the cloth around herself. It didn't seem as secure as Sokdi's; she hoped desperately it wouldn't fall when weighted by water. Sokdi had by now immersed herself in the pool, significantly chillier than Liliana would have preferred, and was happily rubbing a lump of soap into her hair, creating a thick lather that floated downstream.

"It's for your hair." Sokdi smiled, handing the soap to Liliana. Liliana took it gratefully—bathing wasn't on Ardus's list of priorities—the soap smelled heavenly, sweet lavender and sharp citrus. She copied Sokdi, and in spite of the frigid water, it felt wonderful to be clean.

"Now the clothes." Sokdi showed Liliana how to use soap and rocks to wash her clothes, pounding, wringing, then stacking them into a neat pile.

When they finished, Sokdi gave Liliana a dress to wear. It fell past her ankles, dragging on the ground; Sokdi was taller than Liliana, but the dress was clean and fresh. Liliana examined the colorful embroidery covering the skirt. Flowers and birds, interspersed with rippling lines and ribbons of colour.

"Did you make this?" Liliana asked, fingering a pink flower.

"Yes. It's what we all wear at home." Sokdi nodded.

"What are you doing so far from home?" Antarai communities were notoriously independent, rarely leaving the small villages clustered along western mountain ridges to interact with others.

Sokdi gathered the clothing, putting them into her canvas sack.

"We came to speak to King Ruben. An evil creature invaded our land; we're unable to fight it on our own." Sokdi's eyes darkened with sadness.

"Do you mean... a magical creature?" Although Liliana's best friend was a magical cat, she'd never encountered magical creatures of any other kind. Until recently, the royal family outlawed magic in Lovan. Even after King Erich lifted the ban, magic was extremely rare and viewed with profound suspicion by most Lovanians.

Sokdi nodded, worry flitting through her dark eyes.

"What kind of magical creature?" Liliana asked hesitantly.

"An ogre. A shape-shifting ogre." Sokdi hoisted the canvas bag on her shoulder.

Liliana shivered. Ogres were some of the most powerful magical creatures of all, and their unpleasant temperaments made them exceedingly dangerous.

"Have *you* seen the ogre?" Liliana lowered her voice. They were re-entering the campsite.

"No." A hesitant expression crossed Sokdi's face. "But he has." Sokdi slid her eyes toward the man who first discovered Liliana, Tailuk.

Liliana glanced at Tailuk, cheerfully stirring a pot of spicy bean stew over the fire.

"Tailuk almost didn't escape the ogre," Sokdi continued in a whisper. "He was with a hunting group, and he was the only survivor. But Tailuk saw the ogre shift. It had assumed the form of the deer they were hunting and lured them deep into a canyon. The ogre trapped them."

"Why?" Liliana lowered her brows questioningly.

"Who knows? We think for sport or because it was looking for something," Sokdi answered solemnly. "After the ogre killed them, it touched none of the bodies. And," Sokdi paused, "This isn't the only ogre attack. There's been more."

A shiver ran down Liliana's spine. "How will King Erich help with the ogre?"

"King Erich? Of Lovan?" Sokdi drew her brows together, throwing Liliana a questioning look.

"Yes, King Erich. Or is it Princess Lucie, his daughter-in-law you need? The girl who married his son Prince Frederich. She wields the magic sceptre."

"Oh sweetie, we aren't in Lovan, this is Iasia." Sokdi pressed her lips together, holding in a smile.

"It is?" Liliana hadn't realised she had travelled this far. She wondered if Ardus knew they reached Iasia.

"Yes, you're a day and a half walk from the Lovanian border. We're going to see King Ruben. We're hoping he'll use the Iasian sceptre to fight the ogre. It's the only artifact we know of that's powerful enough to defeat ogre magic." Sokdi spread the last item of clothing, a brightly coloured tunic, over a bush.

"Come on, enough talk of ogres; it's depressing. Let's sit by the fire and have dinner. Tailuk's food is amazing." Sokdi took Liliana's hand, leading her to the fire.

Liliana followed Sokdi to a log near the fire, where they handed her a big bowl of spiced rice covered with even spicier stew. Liliana's eyes watered as she took the first bite.

"Oh dear, is it too hot for you? Many people aren't used to eating Antarai food." Sokdi handed Liliana a cup of water.

"No," Liliana choked, gulping the water desperately, face red. "It's delicious. Really. I just wasn't expecting the spice. That's all." She took another tiny bite, this time bracing herself for the sting. After a few mouthfuls, the inferno subsided to a dull burn and Liliana enjoyed the unfamiliar flavours of the strange new food. "Is everything you make like this?" Liliana asked Sokdi, lips still tingling.

"Do you mean spicy?" Sokdi gave her a rueful smile. "Yes."

"It's spicy. But so delicious. So many flavours." The food in Liliana's part of Lovan was good too but very plain, flavoured with salt, butter, and pepper.

Sokdi beamed. "It is very delicious, isn't it? We grow most herbs in our gardens, and we dry them in season so we have them all year round. Here, try some of these; they're good too." She gathered up a pile of steamed leaves that were dark green, interspersed with tiny yellow flowers. Liliana had seen one of the men gathering them when she and Sokdi had gone to bathe. Liliana took a tentative bite.

"Oh, they're good too," Liliana mumbled, mouth full. She'd been expecting a bitter taste, but the leaves were mild, surprisingly tender; sprinkled with salt they provided a welcome contrast to the spicy stew.

"You stay near me," Sokdi told Liliana. "There's all sorts of delicious food in this forest."

Liliana leaned back sleepily, enjoying her full stomach. One of the men brought out a small drum and another an unfamiliar instrument—varying lengths of reeds tied together. He used it to produce a low mournful tune, soon accompanied by singing.

Lulled by the music and the warmth of the fire, Liliana dozed. She only roused her when Sokdi nudged her awake just long enough to guide her to a spare tent where she found her bedroll. Liliana stumbled in, her last memory was the low hum of music and singing as she faded back to sleep.

CHAPTER 14

There was no lingering around the fire the next morning. After a hasty breakfast, a strange porridge substance covered in sticky syrup, the Antarai set off.

"How far are we from Florin?" Liliana asked Sokdi as harnesses jingled. They ambled along the forest paths.

"Three or four days. We're not taking main roads," Sokdi answered.

"Have you been to Florin before?" Liliana glanced at Sokdi, sitting perfectly straight on her pony.

Sokdi shook her head, "No, none of us have. Antarai prefer to stay near home. We're comfortable deep in the mountains. We brought him along," Sokdi pointed out Lukdee who had a mysteriously respected position among the group. He was the oldest there, with long grey hair falling loosely to his shoulders.

Liliana wrinkled her brow, tilting her head toward Sokdi.

"Lukdee is one of the Antarai wise men. A seer," Sokdi explained. "He'll show us the way to Florin."

Liliana had a thousand questions about how seeing worked, but was distracted by the fierce yapping of dogs. The pack had picked up a scent along the path. She and Sokdi quickly pushed to the front of the group. The barking dogs clustered around a fir tree, yapping and jumping. On a high branch, a furious, puffed up and hissing cat crouched.

Liliana scrambled from her pony, running to the tree, shoving through the excited bundle of barking dogs.

"Call them off," Liliana shouted to Lukdee. "That's my cat."

Yingyai, a big burly man with a long braid, whistled shrilly. The dogs slunk back to their place, whining at the imposition.

"You have a cat? Here?" Yingyai furrowed his brow, throwing Liliana a quizzical glance.

"Yes. I have a cat." Not ready to explain why a cat would accompany her on a wilderness journey, Liliana hoisted herself up, climbing the lower branches of the tree.

"Not just *any* cat," Lukdee noted from under the tree, peering through leafy foliage at the angry parcel of fur. "A *magical* cat, hello small friend."

Liliana felt the weight of fifteen pairs of eyes boring into her as she reached through the branches, gently lifting Ardus.

"Hello to you too," Ardus huffed, skipping past Liliana's outstretched hands. He nimbly climbed down from his tree. Ardus sounded distinctly put out, Liliana thought, cautiously sliding down to safety.

"I am, in fact, a magical talking cat; but I do not care to speak to canines." The end of Ardus tail twitched furiously as he stalked the path, carefully avoiding the excited dogs who looked eager to begin the chase again.

"Welcome." Lukdee knelt down until he was eye level with Ardus, the fringe of his embroidered jacket dragging in the dust. "We would be honored if you joined us."

The twitching tail slowed. "Ahem. Well, I suppose, since we're going this direction anyway." The little cat's voice was haughty; his large green eyes blinked furiously. "You have been taking care of my human."

"Would you like to ride with your mistress, fine cat?" Lukdee asked politely.

"She's not my mistress, we're equals." Ardus waited for Liliana to mount back on her pony before vaulting to the front of the saddle, ensconcing himself in place.

"Of course, my mistake," Lukdee's voice was apologetic. He swung back on his mount; and with a jingle of harnesses and whining of dogs, the small group resumed their journey.

"How could you just leave me there, you almost ruined the plan?" Ardus whispered loudly. His back was rigid, voice haughty. Ardus was miffed.

"I thought you wanted to be invisible," Liliana answered. "If I had known you wanted to ride the horse, I would have called you."

"Well. See it doesn't happen again." Ardus turned his back to her, the tilt of his head telling Liliana Ardus hadn't forgiven her.

By lunchtime, Ardus had warmed up to Liliana; and over lunch, he had a long mysterious conversation with Lukdee. Sokdi had produced dried fish and mixed it with rice in a little bowl for Ardus. Bored by conversation consisting primarily of Iasian politics, Liliana wandered away.

"Come with us. We're going to collect mushrooms." Yingyai waved at Liliana from the edge of the path. The ponies needed a rest. It would be awhile before they resumed their journey again.

"Mushrooms?" This intrigued Liliana. She loved her garden but knew little about food foraged from the forest.

"Come, we'll show you," Sokdi urged her.

Besides Yingyai, the group comprised of Sokdi and two others. The conversation was lively, and they laughed and chatted, pushing across scrubby hillsides.

"You find a lot of mushrooms after a heavy rain," Yingyai explained. He pointed to a shaded area around a small beech. Liliana knelt, looking closer. There was a small cluster of mushrooms, small grey balls nestled together.

"Look, there's more." Another cluster was half hidden between two large boulders.

The group worked swiftly, snapping off the tender mushrooms, placing them gently into small baskets hanging from their waist.

"No, don't touch that one," Sokdi's voice rang out in warning.

Liliana snapped her hand back. She peered at the mushroom she had been about to add to her bag. It was creamy white, rimmed with orange.

"That one isn't safe," Sokdi explained. "Do you see, the colour is different. Darker. And there're no insects around it. That's the biggest warning."

"Is it *very* dangerous?" Liliana squinted at the mushrooms, which to her untrained eyes seemed identical. Although now that Sokdi pointed it out, she noticed the variations mentioned.

"That one. Yes. Don't worry." Sokdi laughed at the horrified expression on Liliana's face. "We'll check your mushrooms to make sure nothing harmful slipped in. Just stick with me; I'll make sure you collect the good ones."

After that, Liliana was a more cautious. Forest life was more complicated than she imagined.

"What else can you use from the forest?" Liliana asked Sokdi as they gathered a few more from under a fallen log.

"Out here? Lots of things. Those streams are full of fish, crabs, shrimp, and lots of plants. Lily salad, or soup is delicious. There are other edible plants too. And the Iasian game is wonderful. Scarcer here than the thick forest, but worth the effort."

Liliana scanned the area. It seemed like a wasteland of weeds and branches to her untrained eyes.

"I'll teach you as we go along." Sokdi sat back on her heels, tucking her colourful skirt around her. "If you're going to survive in the wild, you need to learn to use all the resources available. Yingyai is the best trapper of all the Antarai. He'll show you how to trap a grouse and other birds. He even trapped a firebird once." Sokdi's eyes widened in appreciation.

"Firebirds are real?" With their baskets full, the mushroom gatherers began heading back to the path.

Yingyai shot Liliana a grin. "Of course, firebirds are real."

"What did you do with the firebird?" Liliana always thought firebirds were long-extinct mythical creatures.

"Let it go free. Too precious to eat. The bird gave me this, though. A gift." Yingyai reached under his shirt, pulling out a gleaming chain. On the end of it hung a single feather. Even in the blazing sunlight, Liliana could see it emitted a strange, unearthly glow of its own.

"Amazing. Can I touch it?" When Yingyai nodded, Liliana reached out a finger to touch the feather. It was soft and light, sliding through her fingers like satin.

"How does the feather not get damaged?" the feather was so delicate, Liliana wondered how it remained intact.

"Firebird feathers are indestructible. It's said if you get one as a gift, it gives you good luck."

Liliana watched Yingyai slide the feather into place. "Does it help you with trapping?"

"Exactly." Yingyai winked, giving his feather a satisfied pat.

They reached the path where the rest of the party waited patiently, already mounted on their ponies.

"Come. We continue to Florin." Lukdee gestured.

AFTER SEVERAL DAYS of travel, Liliana felt at home with the Antarai. She was having more fun than she'd ever had in her life. Sokdi took her under her wing, and with the other Antarai, she taught Liliana the ways of forest life. It fascinated Liliana to no end. Ardus joined her in the borrowed bedroll at night, and when it rained, the group set up two large tents that held all of them.

Although the terrain was rough, they were seeing signs of civilisation. First, a few farms, eking out a living on the sparse ground, raising sheep and a tough, hardy breed of goat. The creatures were unfamiliar to Liliana who was used to the gentle lowland farm animals. Then, the hills flattened, and they arrived in the first town.

By now, Liliana was accustomed to the dress and ways of the Antarai, so the suspicious glances people gave the party as their shaggy ponies jingled through town, irked her to no end.

"How can you stand it?" she asked Lukdee as they sat next to the crackling fire.

"Oh, people don't like anything different from themselves." The townspeople's opinions hadn't bothered Lukdee. This too, was strange to Liliana. In Annecy, social standing and people's judgements were crucial. Liliana was used to putting great significance on people's opinions.

"We reach the outskirts of Florin tonight," Sokdi told Liliana as they folded bedrolls the next morning. The news disconcerted Liliana. She realized she loved the Antarai world and wasn't ready to part with them yet.

Sure enough, that evening, they drew close to Florin, camping in a charming meadow on a hill, the towers of the castle rising in the distance.

"We're trapping first thing in the morning," Yingyai told her that night.

Liliana jumped out her bedroll at the first birdsong. She slipped into a pair of colourful embroidered breeches and a flowing tunic provided by Sokdi and grabbed some cold flatbread.

Yingyai waited by the fire.

"Are you ready?" Yingyai whispered. Most of the party were still asleep. The instruments had appeared last night; the Antarai were tired from singing.

Liliana followed Yingyai as he silently left the campsite. Hearing a rustle, she turned around. Padding behind her was a small furry body, the grey fur blending in with the predawn light.

"Are you coming too?" she asked Ardus.

"Of course, I'm coming. Cats are the best hunters, you know?" Tail erect, the cat kept pace as they trotted down steep paths, winding through the hillsides.

The trio walked steadily until they reached a woodland area. Yingyai held up his hand. "Stop here." He backed into the underbrush, crouching low. Liliana squatted beside him, hissing as thorny vines scraped through her clothes.

"Don't you need a trap?" Liliana whispered loudly. Yingyai put his finger to his lips, signalling for Liliana to be quiet, shaking his head. Liliana's feet grew numb. She wasn't as limber and flexible as the Antarai; tingling pins and needles spread up her legs, begging her to move. Just when she felt she couldn't bear it, Yingyai pursed his lips and called. He made a low cooing sound, accompanied by scraping and scratching on the ground. Liliana watched, riveted.

Soon, Liliana heard rustling in the bushes. Transfixed, Liliana hardly dared breathe as Yingyai kept calling until a fat grouse emerged. The grouse was so close, Liliana could count every line in his patterned feathers. He came closer, pecking and scratching the woodland floor.

There was a flash of movement.

Yingyai shot out his arm, and it was over. Yingyai cradled the grouse gently in his arms. The animal was confused more than distressed by its capture as it rested in the crook of Yingyai's elbow. Yingyai popped the grouse into his basket and fitted the lid securely over it.

Wide-eyed, Liliana followed Yingyai as he captured two more of birds before he was satisfied.

"Could I learn how to trap birds like that?" Liliana asked Yingyai as they pushed through the thick spiky underbrush.

Yingyai paused, hand still on the prickly branch he was pulling back to allow Liliana through. "Of course, you can learn. I mean, it takes time to get really good. But trapping's not that hard. I'll take you out a few more times before you try trapping solo."

When they reached the campsite, Yingyai tossed the grouse a handful of oats before setting the basket aside. The grouse were content as they pecked and munched away at their oats. Breakfast was ready, and Liliana hungrily dug into the strange porridge, which by now she was getting used to. The porridge wasn't so bad when you added toppings. Today's toppings consisted of of salted meat, fried until crispy and a chopped wild onions to sprinkle over it.

Sokdi and Lukdee sat beside Liliana, gracefully bending their legs underneath them in a cross-legged position.

"Good morning." Liliana gulped her porridge. Sokdi's expression told Liliana she had something important to say.

"We were wondering if you would do us a favour." Sokdi hesitated.

"Yes. Anything." Liliana smiled, eager to repay the Antarai for all their generosity.

"We were wondering if you and Ardus would be willing to present the grouse to King Ruben and Queen Abigail for us. As a goodwill gift."

Liliana glanced from Sokdi to Lukdee, confusion swimming in her eyes. "If it's a goodwill gift, don't you want King Ruben to know it's from you? Does the royal family even like grouse."

"Oh yes. King Ruben loves grouse. But we need to put our case before him in the best possible light."

"Of course." Liliana still didn't understand how her bringing King Ruben a gift would help the Antarai gain favour. But she trusted Sokdi; she was happy to try it.

"Here, wear this." Sokdi poked through a pack, contents strewn around her. She held out a long, embroidered jacket, colourful patterns and flowers covering every inch of the fabric. Liliana hesitated. In her Annecy life, she always dressed to blend in. That outfit would ensure every eye was was trained firmly on her.

"Go on." Sokdi gave the jacket a shake. Liliana put the jacket on. The sleeves were a little long, but otherwise, it fit perfectly, its billowing hem nearly touching the ground as it flared out behind her. Liliana swung her arms experimentally. She had to admit, this was a lot more comfortable than the usual laced up dresses she wore.

"I'll fix your hair." Sokdi took a wooden comb and sat Liliana down on a flat rock. Soon, Liliana's hair was wrapped in an intricate braid circling her head and pinned securely with enamel combs.

"There. Ready." Sokdi smiled in satisfaction.

Liliana felt the smooth braid as she ran her fingers over the cool, smooth enamel.

Tailuk raised his eyebrows approvingly when Liliana and Sokdi emerged from the tent.

"Ready?" he asked, tossing Liliana a grin.

"As I'll ever be." Liliana mounted her pony, tucking the jacket in around her.

"Wait for me," a huffy feline voice puffed behind her. Liliana turned. There was Ardus, wearing the hat and the boots.

"I don't know how you humans stand these horrible things on your feet all the time. It makes it so much harder to do anything. Maybe that's why your so clumsy," Ardus complained as Liliana lifted him into the saddle in front of her.

"You look very handsome." Liliana held in a smile. Ardus was exceedingly dapper in his tiny leather boots and hat with the curling feather.

"Humph," the little cat replied as he primly tucked his tail underneath him.

The Iasian castle was farther than it appeared. It was midday by the time the small party arrived. First, they encountered the guard, who carefully removed Tailuk's large curling knife and set it aside, assuring him he would return it when he left the castle grounds. He then directed them to the audience hall, a large airy room.

Iasian citizens crowded the audience hall, packing the room until they spilled over the seating area, lining the wall. Unsure of the protocol, Liliana was glad for a chance to observe.

After a long wait, it was their turn. Tailuk held Liliana back.

"Ardus is presenting," Tailuk whispered.

"Wait, aren't we all presenting?" Liliana shot Tailuk a nervous look, wondering what the little cat planned to say to King Ruben and Queen Abigail.

"No, Ardus knows exactly what to do." Tailuk smiled encouragingly, his hand warm on Liliana's arm.

Nervously, Liliana watched as the little cat proudly made his way down the aisle toward the dais. She felt the stares of people and heard more than a few whispers follow him as Ardus stalked toward King Ruben and Queen Abigail. They watched him approach with an amused expression.

King Ruben and Queen Abigail were seated on giant gilded seats, intricately carved with mythical creatures. When he reached them, the little cat bowed deeply in front of them, the feather on his hat brushing the marble floor.

"Your majesties." The little cat's feather bobbed elegantly as he bowed again. He stalked toward the king and queen, who watched him with an amused expression. Liliana trained her eyes straight ahead, knowing if she heard what they were saying, she would lose her courage and make a grab for the brave little cat.

CHAPTER 15

"Well, how delightful." Queen Abigail's pleased smile lit up her face.

"I come on behalf of the Marquis of Carabas," the cat spoke politely, sweeping an elegant bow.

"Marquis of Carabas?" Queen Abigail turned to King Ruben, questions in her eyes. "Now who is that?" Liliana hovered on the edge of her seat. What was Ardus doing now? She'd never heard of the Marquis of Carabas.

"From the Western Mountains, your majesties," Ardus continued smoothly, ignoring everyone's surprise. "My mistress prefers the quiet, secluded life."

"Oh, I see." King Ruben grinned, eyes twinkling with curiosity. "Well, you're very welcome on behalf of our Marquis."

"Thank you, Your Majesty. My mistress asked us to send this small token of appreciation." The cat gestured grandly toward Tailuk, who carried the basket holding the three grouse, still clucking and content from their morning feed.

"Oh, lovely, that was very nice of the Marquis indeed." King Ruben leaned forward, eagerly peering through the slats of the basket. "I must add them to my collection in the garden. I've never seen that exact pattern before."

The cat bowed again. Tailuk following suit with a bow of his own, not quite as elegant as the little cat's.

Acutely aware of the stares and whispers, Liliana stumbled to the entrance of the hall where Tailuk and Ardus waited for her. Tailuk raised his chin, gesturing for Liliana to follow, heading briskly toward the outer courtyard.

And then it happened. Liliana had scooped Ardus in her arms and was busy removing his hat and boots, when suddenly a large object smacked into her. Liliana sprawled to the floor.

"Excuse me." Liliana looked up, expecting castle staff, but instead found a pair of familiar green eyes studying on her.

"Pardon me miss." Prince Landry grinned, holding a hand to help her up.

"I'm so sorry," Liliana stammered, fiery blush heating her cheeks. Landry wasn't alone. Next to him was a girl. A beautiful girl. Tall, slender, regal, wearing a gorgeous dress. Liliana's face grew redder as the girl curled her lip, drawing back her skirts.

"It was my fault. I wasn't watching where I was going." Landry ignored the girl as he knelt to gather his scattered papers, bundling them into an untidy stack. "I hope you didn't get hurt." Landry paused, meeting Liliana's eyes.

Temporarily mesmerized by the deep green of his eyes, Liliana lost her train of thought. "Er, yes. I'm fine," she stammered, hoping he didn't think she was a complete ninny. Landry's companion was visibly impatient, tapping her velvet slippered foot and rolling her eyes.

Liliana picked up the last few papers, handing them to Landry, drawing back quickly as their fingers touched. Landry's hands were warm and rough. A tingle went through Liliana at the unexpected contact.

"Thank you." Landry tucked the papers under his arm and stood, right in Liliana's path. Not wanting to ask him to move, Liliana waited in awkward silence for him to say something. Anything.

"I don't believe we've met." Landry ignored his irritable companion and smiled, showing a dimple in one cheek.

"I'm Liliana." She held her breath, hoping he wouldn't remember their awkward encounter at the market.

Landry took Liliana's small hand in his. "A pleasure."

"Come on, Landry. I don't want to be late for our walk. We were to meet Celine and Alex." The girl tugged Landry's arm.

After holding Liliana's hand for another brief moment, Landry glanced down, suddenly remembering he was holding it.

"Well, it was lovely to meet you, Liliana." Landry winked, moving down the corridor. His companion tucked her hand in his arm, leaning to whisper in Landry's ear as they strolled away.

Dazed, Liliana picked up the cat and his accessories, running to catch up with Tailuk, waiting at the end of the hall for them.

"Who was that?" Tailuk asked.

"Prince Landry, and... someone?" Liliana didn't know the girl, only that she didn't care to meet her again.

"I see." Tailuk smirked, raising an eyebrow. "Isn't he the prince that's still single?"

"Yes, apparently not for long," Liliana grumbled, wondering what Tailuk was getting at. Clearly, she and Prince Landry moved in different worlds. Liliana sighed as Tailuk collected his knife, examining it carefully for scratches before sliding it back into his waistband.

CHAPTER 16

"Psst. Psst." Groaning, Liliana rolled over. The fire had died to glowing coals. The grey light told Liliana that it was early.

"What is it?" Liliana groaned again, poking her nose out of her bedroll.

Yingyai put a finger to his lips, signalling for Liliana to be quiet.

"Come with me," he whispered.

Mumbling complaints under her breath, Liliana pulled on her boots and followed Yingyai as he led her north.

"Where are we going?" she asked him, out of earshot of the campsite.

"I discovered a litter of Hardeen wolves. I wanted to show you."

"Aren't Hardeen wolves dangerous?" Liliana froze mid-step.

"Not if you do things right," Yingyai's voice exuded confidence. "Something may have happened to the Hardeen wolf mother. I didn't see the wolf all day yesterday; I need to check if she returned. It's unusual for wolf pups to be left alone more than an hour. If they're alone, I'm going to collect them."

"Oh, they're still babies?"

"Yes. If you hand raise a Hardeen, they're loyal guard dogs. Very protective and devoted to a fault."

Liliana followed Yingyai as he led her over a series of boulder-strewn hills. When they arrived at a spot under an overhanging rock, Yingyai signalled for Liliana to hang back. Stealthily creeping along the side of the rock, he approached a small opening and disappeared inside. Moments later, Yingyai emerged, waving Liliana on, and she scrambled over to him. The opening led to a narrow cave. In the middle of the cave was a furry pile of squirming Hardeen pups.

"Oh, they're so small." The wolf pups bore no resemblance to the wolves that left giant footprints surrounding the cabin in the woods. Liliana held out a hand and one of the puppies sniffed it cautiously before sucking vigorously on her finger.

"He's hungry." She giggled at the tickling sensation.

"Yes, Sokdi will have milk to give them." Yingyai lifted the squirming bundles of fur, setting them gently on a blanket laid on the bottom of the basket.

The puppies yipped in surprise as he lifted the basket, but soon settled into their wriggling pile.

When they arrived back at camp, Sokdi was warming a small pan of milk obtained from a nearby farm. When it was ready, she set it in the basket and the wolf pups eagerly gathered around, slurping until their small tummies were taught and full.

"What will you do with them?" Liliana stroked one of the pups, who chewed her finger happily in response.

"Well, we'll raise them. If they want to return to the forest when they're grown, they can, but this one." Sokdi lifted one of the larger pups out. "This one is for King Ruben." The pup kicked his little legs and Sokdi set him back down.

"Another trip to the castle?" Sokdi smiled at Liliana.

CHAPTER 17

Liliana straightened her colourful jacket and smoothed her hands over her hair. Liliana still wasn't comfortable being the centre of attention, but she was learning to ignore the curious stares and judgy remarks. It was a few days after Yingyai had gotten the pups; Sokdi wanted to build the pup to full health before presenting it to King Ruben.

Taking a deep breath, Liliana lifted the basket, wriggling pup inside, and the trio approached the guard. Tailuk handed over his knife with hardly a grumble. They went in, finding seats at the back of the audience hall.

When their turn arrived, Liliana straightened her spine, watching Ardus saunter up the long aisle toward the dais. Today, three others accompanied King Ruben and Queen Abigail. Liliana immediately recognized the famous golden hair of Princess Celine and Prince Alex next to her. Liliana's eyes skipped to the opposite side of the dais. A pair of familiar green eyes met hers. Prince Landry's companion was missing from the party, a fact that gave Liliana a bigger thrill of satisfaction than it should have.

Ardus bowed low in a sweeping gesture.

"Your majesties," the little cat's tone was formal and polite.

"It pleases the Marquis of Carabas to send you this gift." Ceremoniously, Ardus waved a paw at the basket Tailuk carried to the front of the hall. A tiny black nose poked through the slats, followed by a pink tongue.

"A dog?" King Ruben furrowed his brow.

"Ah. Not just a dog. A Heerdan wolf. He will grow up to be your most loyal and faithful companion. With a Heerdan wolf at your side, you will need no guards; he will be matchless in strength and speed." Feather trembling slightly with the fervour of his words, Ardus waxed eloquent on the virtues of the little pup.

By now, Queen Abigail had lifted the pup out of his basket, and the queen's small companion dog was sniffing suspiciously at him, growling at the back of its tiny throat. The pup paid no notice, wagging its floppy tail, already sprouting tufts of grey fluff.

Celine leaned forward to inspect the pup. "I've heard about the Heerdan wolf; aren't they the ones that fought beside us in battles?" She reached out a finger which the little wolf licked with enthusiasm, pink stubby tongue flickering in and out energetically.

"Let me look at him." Prince Landry cradled the dog in his hand, stroking its ears that still had his baby floppiness. When the wolf got older, the ears would prick up.

The little wolf settled in Landry's arms, panting happily. "I think we should call him Bardolf." The wolf snuggled in a furry ball against his chest. She couldn't believe this pup was one of the fiercest carnivores on the continent.

"Well, it looks like little Bardolf has found himself a new home." King Ruben smiled. "Thank you for the splendid gift. And of course, give our best to your master, the Marquis."

Ardus tipped his head gracefully in acknowledgement, and Tailuk bowed. They turned, Liliana following but not before she glimpsed green eyes lingering on her face.

"Do you think they like the Heerden?" Tailuk handed Liliana the reins to her pony.

"They loved it." She settled herself into the saddle, Ardus perched primly front of her. "But I don't understand how this helps with the ogre problem. Has Lukdee told you his plans yet?"

Tailuk smiled. "Lukdee's always kept his plans secretive. He says too many variables change the outcome. We've learned he's usually right, so we trust him."

Liliana considered this, riding in silence. "Has he told you what the next step is?"

Tailuk shook his head, unbothered. "No."

It wasn't until a few days later that Liliana got another morning wake-up call. She sleepily got out of the bedroll.

"We're taking ponies this time," Yingyai whispered, "It's farther today."

Liliana saddled her mount and fell in behind Yingyai. "What are we hunting for this time?" she asked, drawing her hood further over her head. It was raining, a soft fine mist permeating the air with dampness.

"We're not hunting, we're collecting. It's a lindwurm skin. One started shedding yesterday; she should be finished by now."

Liliana's jaw dropped. Lindwurms were notoriously dangerous, half the size of dragons, but just as fierce. She had seen pictures of them. Terrifying. Large snakelike creatures with tiny arms and huge poisonous fangs.

"They're real? Isn't this going to be dangerous?"

Yingyai chuckled. "Yes. And yes. But follow me and you'll be fine. Look, I brought you this."

Yingyai handed Liliana a large, curved knife, similar to the one tucked into his waistband. Only instead of a shining black handle, this one was silver, carved with intricate patterns of flowers and leaves.

Liliana hesitated. "I don't know how to use knives."

Yingyai grinned. "You'll figure it out. Be careful with it; it's been dipped." He noticed her confused look and explained. "Dipped in poison. I don't plan to encounter the Lindwurm, but if I do, that will kill it in minutes."

Liliana tucked the knife carefully into the loop on her waistband, making sure the blade stayed in its cover.

The surefooted ponies headed into the steep hills leading away from the capital. Higher and higher they climbed, stopping only for a hasty breakfast, dried fish and flatbread baked over the coals the previous day.

"Another hour," Yingyai announced cheerfully as they remounted the horses. A few hills later, Yingyai stopped his pony, turning to Liliana.

"We'll leave the ponies here and travel on foot. We don't want to startle the Lindwurm."

Leaving the horses to forage in the scrubby grass that covered the hillside, they set off, climbing over boulders and pushing through underbrush. Yingyai turned, motioning for Liliana to move quietly as he crouched low, brown cloak blending into the underbrush. Liliana followed, although more noisily.

Yingyai led Liliana to a depression of flattened grass; there it was, the Lindwurm skin—a shimmer of scales in the morning sun. Liliana caught her breath. It was huge. Yingyai scanned the area, checking that their way was clear. He carefully spread out the Lindwurm skin until it lay flat, then together they worked to fold it. The skin held the shape of the individual scales, roughly the size of Liliana's hand. The scales caught the light in a flashing rainbow of color. Liliana felt the magic seeping from the Lindwurm skin, coating the air in tingling layers, so thick she could almost breathe it in.

Soon, the skin was a neat pile and Yingyai produced a cloth which he wrapped gently around the skin, forming a tidy package tied with twine. They still hadn't spoken a word, working in complete silence, but Yingyai smiled as he lifted the package, leading Liliana from the clearing.

A feeling of relief washed over Liliana as they left the patch of flattened grass, but she hadn't taken more than three steps when she heard a loud rumbling. Her eyes widened as the ground in front of her shifted, rising. Chunks of earth fell away as a large snout with fierce beady eyes emerged from the rocky soil. Liliana screamed as the creature rose higher and higher, preparing to strike.

"Run!" shouted Yingyai.

Liliana turned and sprinted.

She tripped over loose rocks and branches, but somehow remaining upright, somehow moving forward.

The rumbling behind Liliana grew louder. More violent. There was a scrabbling, shuffling noise getting closer. The Lindwurm was using his arms to dig himself out of the soil. Liliana's legs pumped hard, a pain shot through her side as she gasped for breath.

Something knocked Liliana to the side. She fell to her hands and knees. The impact sent jolts of pain through everything. Liliana looked up, craning her neck. Rearing against the sky, the Lindwurm was immense and very, very angry. The fangs glinted as the creature opened its mouth, letting out a loud cry, keening and howling.

There was no point in running. This creature was impossibly big and fast, but still Liliana gathered her legs and leaping forward with all her might. The Lindwurm struck, narrowly missing Liliana as it rattled its teeth on the rock she had fallen on. Liliana could smell its breath, like rotten meat, as she scrambled desperately over the boulders.

The Lindwurm screeched, rearing to strike again, but something distracted it, giving Liliana a chance to scramble underneath the lip of an overhanging rock. Not that it would help. The Lindwurm were excellent diggers, living in underground burrows that they scraped out with sharp claws.

The creature hissed, twisting to look behind itself. Liliana flattened herself onto the rock. The creature seemed to have forgotten Liliana, concentrating on something behind it. Liliana looked again; Yingyai was striking the creature with his large knife, dancing out of range of the venomous fangs.

The creature shrieked and dove again, giving Liliana the chance to pull out her borrowed knife. Gripping the handle with both hands, she stepped from beneath her rock. The Lindwurm was facing away, exposing its side. Seeing a soft spot where the scales spread less thickly, Liliana took aim and struck.

The Lindwurm hissed, turning back to her, and Liliana slid under her rock just in time. She felt tugging. The fangs caught her sleeve, but Liliana yanked hard, ripping it from the creature's jaws.

The deadly dance continued. Liliana got in another strike, piercing the thick hide. She saw the creature was slowing down, appearing confused, weaving its head back and forth between Liliana and Yingyai until finally it flopped down, shaking the earth with a thud. A few rocks broke free, rolled down the hill, and clattered into the distance. Liliana hesitated a minute before emerging from her hiding place.

Yingyai sat on the ground, breathing hard.

"Are you all right?" Liliana put a hand on his shoulder. His tunic was damp with sweat.

Yingyai looked up at Liliana, his contagious grin firmly in place.

"That was amazing," Yingyai's voice was filled with awe.

"Well, that's definitely one way of putting it," Liliana commented wryly as she shakily wiped her knife on some dried grass.

"You were fantastic." Yingyai cleaned his own knife before sliding it into his waistband.

"I could never have gotten the Lindwurm without you. Of course." He added with a cheeky grin, "It probably wouldn't have heard any noises if it were just me." Yingyai ducked as Liliana cuffed him playfully.

Yingyai collected the Lindwurm skin, none the worse for its adventure, and they began their descent. That evening around the campfire, Liliana felt she belonged like never before. Yingyai found great pleasure in telling the story of how Liliana had helped him defeat the Lindwurm, and she basked in the glow of a job well done. She was actually looking forward to presenting the gift to King Ruben.

Lindwurm skins were renowned for medicinal properties; Liliana knew the generous gift would benefit the Iasians.

Sokdi took extra care with Liliana's hair the next morning. Leaving it down, she brushed it into shining waves falling around Liliana's shoulders. Sokdi tucked a new comb in Liliana's hair, a shining dragon etched into the colorful enamel.

"After all, you're a warrior now," Sokdi commented, smoothing gentle hands down the glossy length one last time.

Liliana cleaned the mud off her boots, and once again donned her embroidered jacket. With Ardus perched in front of her and accompanied by Tailuk, she began her journey to the castle.

They were halfway there when she saw them. A group of ten, heading out on a pleasure ride, saddlebags bulging with picnic fare. Liliana saw glass lemonade bottles peeking from one bag and a sheaf of crusty loaves from another.

It wasn't unusual to pass travellers this close to Florin, but this was obviously a royal party. Liliana noted the crest on the horses and the guards accompanying them. She glimpsed Celine, her hair flying behind her like a golden banner. Landry's companion from the day before was next to her, dressed in a splendid, rich riding habit.

Liliana and Tailuk politely moved to the edge of the road to let the party pass. But to her surprise, they halted. Liliana waited, hand stroking Ardus's fur, wondering why they were stopping. Prince Alex and Prince Landry conversed with each other, leaning over the necks of their horses, whispering. Prince Landry's companion was nearby, a frown marring her pretty face. Landry glanced more than once at Liliana, his green eyes locking with hers. Then they rode away in a flurry of hoofbeats.

Liliana took a deep breath, trying to steady her beating heart.

"Will we continue?" She turned to Tailuk, who was considering her with a curious expression.

This time, the guard recognized them. Waving them through, he sent them on to the audience hall. Again, Tailuk and Liliana held back while Ardus went forward when the aide called them.

"Ah, you again." The King smiled at the little cat who bowed ostentatiously.

"And what brings you this time? A Pheonix? A Firebird?" King Ruben was cut short by a nudge and warning look from his wife.

"Ahem. You're most welcome," the king corrected himself, speaking formally to the little cat.

"Your Majesty, unfortunately, I do not have a Phoenix or a Firebird to present you. But I pray you accept this humble gift instead. From my master, the Marquis of Carabas." The cat gestured to Tailuk, who presented a package wrapped in a finely embroidered silk cloth.

The King's eyes lit up with curiosity; even Queen Abigail leaned forward, alert to see what wondrous object the mysterious packet contained.

"A Lindwurm skin."

The people in the front row gasped, leaning forward to peer at the mysterious packet. It was a well-known fact, acquiring a Lindwurm skin was a perilous and difficult task.

The king tipped his head, signalling for Tailuk to unwrap the cloth.

Everyone held their breath as the cloth slid away, revealing the Lindwurm skin. Shimmering flecks of light danced across the polished floor. Tingling magic filtered through the room—Liliana felt it shiver over her skin like a cool lavender breeze.

"Beautiful and useful." Gratitude shone from the king's eyes. "I'll have it sent to the castle infirmary for safekeeping immediately." Tailuk carefully wrapped the package, placing it gently in the hands of one a waiting castle aide.

The cat bowed again, turning to leave.

"Wait." King Ruben held up his hand. "I must admit, I'm exceedingly curious about this Marquis of Carabas. I've had the court scholars research the matter. It appears the Marquis and his family retreated to the mountain, disappearing from court two hundred years ago if I'm not mistaken. How is it they've returned?"

"Your Majesty, that is a matter not mine to discuss," Ardus' cat voice was apologetic but firm.

"Well, please inform the Marquis he's welcome at the castle? I am most eager to make his acquaintance."

The little cat tipped his head. "I will bring your invitation to my *Mistress*."

The king raised an eyebrow and Queen Abigail's eyes followed the little cat as he retreated.

"That went well." Tailuk smiled as they met Ardus outside the door of the audience hall.

"What went well?" Liliana knelt, helping Ardus remove the boots.

"They're dying with curiosity." Ardus answered, rested in Liliana's arms. "We're ready for the next step."

"Next step?" Liliana questioned.

Ardus batted a paw. "I'll explain later," he informed her mysteriously.

Liliana rolled her eyes, following Tailuk to the courtyard where he collected his knife.

"I still don't understand this plan. Can't you just ask King Ruben to help with the ogre? He seems interested in the welfare of the people. Not like your last queen." Liliana wrinkled her nose in disgust. Even Lovanians knew Queen Penelope had taken advantage of her people in despicable ways to advance personal interests. Personal interests including a plot to take over Lovan. A plan thwarted by brave Princess Lucie and Prince Frederich.

"We could," Tailuk admitted, "and I know he would help us. But sometimes it's better to plant in season." He exchanged a mysterious glance with Ardus.

Liliana wrinkled her brow, and Tailuk laughed. "It's a saying. It means to take your time so you get the best result. You'll see."

Liliana tipped her head thoughtfully. Pretending the gifts were from the Marquis made no sense to her—but she trusted Ardus, and she trusted the Antarai.

"Well," the cat's bossy voice interrupted Liliana's thoughts. "Are we staying here all day? Let's go back to camp."

When they returned, Lukdee ushered Tailuk off for a private conversation. When they came back, they were smiling.

"We leave tomorrow," Lukdee announced that night over dinner. Liliana felt a dart of dread shoot through her. Where did this leave her?

"Where are you going?" she whispered to Sokdi, sitting next to her, eating the savoury stew Yingyai had produced for dinner.

"Home." Sokdi dipped her bread in the stew.

The dread grew as Liliana wondered what she would do without the Antarai. She had felt like part of the group. Sokdi paused, noticing Liliana's distress.

"What's wrong?" she asked, turning to Liliana.

"I'm going to miss all of you." Liliana tried unsuccessfully to keep the tremble out of her voice.

"Aren't you joining us?" Sokdi set her plate on her knee.

Hope flared in Liliana's chest. "I am?"

"Of course you are silly." Sokdi laughed. "We're all expecting you to."

"Oh, um, I didn't know." Liliana dropped her eyes. A weight rolled off her shoulders.

Sokdi put her hand on Liliana's arm. "You're one of us now. I'm sorry none of us ever thought to even tell you," she said to the other girl.

Liliana leaned back, absorbing this new idea.

"Now, eat your dinner; I'm going to need some help washing up when you're done." Sokdi mopped up her last bit of stew, popping the bread in her mouth.

That night, Liliana curled in her bedroll, listening to the gentle rain patter on the canvas, wondered where her life was leading. She thought about what she left behind. Gavin, the mills, her new niece or nephew. Finally, warmed by the furry body of her little cat, she fell fast asleep.

They packed swiftly in the morning, rolling the tents and organizing the ponies. After a quick breakfast, more porridge, they set off.

They travelled west, heading toward Nanves, the last town before the western mountain ranges. Two days later, they arrived.

The town was small, nestled against towering snow-capped mountains. But in spite of its size, the townspeople were well used to provisioning travelers undertaking the arduous journey west. Liliana glanced around Market Square in delight. It was so different from Annecy, where the same traders sold the same wares—mostly vegetables and other food items. Liliana relished the variety.

"Can I look around?" Liliana asked Sokdi, anxious to see and experience everything.

Sokdi laughed. "Of course, we're planning to stay in Nanves a few days. I love the market here; I'll join you."

Together, they looked at the wares various merchants offered, piles of spices, dried food, some very mysterious indeed, and everything else a traveller might need to undertake a long journey.

"What's this?" Liliana pointed to a stall where a merchant was boiling dark coloured liquid over a copper brazier in a shiny copper pot.

"Coffee." Sokdi glanced at the stall. "An acquired taste, but you can try some if you want." Sokdi nodded to the vender, who poured the steaming liquid into a tiny cup, handing it to Liliana with a smile.

Liliana blew on the liquid before sipping carefully. "It's bitter." She screwed up her face.

The vender laughed. "Here, add this." He tonged in three lumps of course brown sugar, stirring them into the cup. Liliana tasted the liquid again. Better. Liliana savoured the coffee, drinking half of it before Sokdi pulled her away. Thanking the vendor, Liliana followed Sokdi deeper into Market Square, stopping for Sokdi to peruse an array of colourful thread.

Sokdi took her time examining the thread, and Liliana began to fidget. Another stall caught her eye, this one selling colourful glass items. She wandered closer, admiring how the light shone through the multi-coloured glass.

"I hear they're all touring this year." The glass merchant, sporting a colourful turban and long robes, nodded, briefly acknowledging Liliana before turning back to his companion.

"I suppose they have to introduce the new princess." The man's friend, similarly dressed, made himself comfortable on the stool behind the wooden table.

"Are you sure King Ruben's coming this way first?" the other merchant asked, swigging cider from a large wooden cup.

"That's what Kian the innkeeper said. Only Queen Abigail is staying in Florin."

The merchant shook his head, tutting. "They're sitting ducks with all that's going on in the Western mountains. I hope they came well-guarded."

Sokdi waved to Liliana, and she left the glass vender, wondering what danger they were referring to in the Western mountains. Had news of the Ogre reached Nanves; if so, it must be serious. No wonder the Antarai needed King Ruben's help.

Mind buzzing with questions, Liliana joined Sokdi, who had a large package tucked under her arm.

"For embroidery. I'm going to sew you a dress," Sokdi explained. "There's a fabric stall. Do you want to come with me to choose?"

Touched that Sokdi would spend so much time on a kind gesture, Liliana accompanied her to the fabric stall, choosing a deep blue material. Laden with purchases, the two rejoined the Antarai group.

"We're staying in Nanves this week," Sokdi explained as they set up camp in a nearby wooded area. The ground was rough, the trees grew sparse here. Liliana joined the Antarai, picking up the larger rocks, providing a smooth place to sleep. Ardus presided over the camp, smoothing his whiskers with his paws as Tailuk lit the campfire.

Over the week, Liliana kept busy as the Antarai, in turns, took her into the hills, teaching her to hunt and forage. Liliana was so busy that she didn't notice the town bustling, all preparing for the impending arrival of the royal family's kingdom tour. The windows on every house were polished until they sparkled, the streets swept clean, every hedge, every garden immaculate. The marketplace buzzed with whispers and speculation as they anticipated the royal arrival with great excitement.

It was amazing what you could find in the forest, Liliana thought proudly as she confidently selected mushrooms from around the base of a fir tree. They would taste good grilled over the fire. She tucked the mushrooms into her basket.

"I never see you anymore," complained Ardus after she presented her findings to Tailuk. He was in charge of dinner that evening.

"I'm sorry." Liliana lifted the small cat in her arms, tickling his chin.

"Well, tomorrow you're coming with me," announced the cat. "It's all arranged. I'm taking you swimming."

"Swimming?" Liliana slid Ardus a questioning look. In her experience, Ardus was not a fan of large bodies of water.

"Yes, swimming in the river, tomorrow's going to be warm enough." The little cat purred as Liliana stroked his furry head. "But, you have to listen to everything I say. And no questions."

"All right. I'll go swimming with you." Liliana laughed at Ardus's insisting tone.

The next morning, the sun shone brightly, infusing the air with warmth. Liliana breathed in the scent of pine and warm earth as she followed Ardus to the swimming spot he'd found. The little cat was right, it was a pleasant spot. A small sandy beach leading to a pool of still clear water, although near the road. Trees surrounding the pool provided privacy from casual travellers.

Delighted, Liliana took out her bathing skirt, wrapping it confidently around herself. Neatly folding the rest of her clothes, she left them in a small pile on a flat rock and waded into the pool.

The water was chilly, but Liliana soon got used to it and began washing her hair with the bar of soap Sokdi gave her, inhaling the sweet floral scent as she lathered it into her hair. She dipped her head under the water, squeezing the water out. It was then she noticed. The clothes were gone. The rock was bare. Liliana looked around, frantically hoping she was mistaken. Maybe she had put them on a different rock?

A slight, almost imperceptible swish caught her attention. She looked over and with disbelief, Liliana watched Ardus, her friend and trusted companion, dragging her shoe into the water. Liliana desperately attempted to rescue the shoe before it reached the swirling current, but she was too late.

Liliana watched helplessly as the shoe bobbed and circled a large rock midstream before the water swept it away. Liliana was too weak a swimmer to reach it. Hair dripping, Liliana furiously faced the little cat who had resumed his position on the rock, an unrepentant expression on the furry face.

"What were you thinking?" Waist deep, icy water dripping down her back, Liliana frowned at the cat who was licking the stray droplets of water off his grey coat.

"I know. You're upset. But wait and see. This is in your best interest." Ardus flicked an ear.

"How is it in my best interest?" Liliana demanded, eyes sparkling with anger. "And why wait and see. No one tells me anything and I'm getting fed up."

Ardus tried—and failed to look apologetic. "I know, it's a lot to expect, but I need you to play along. Then I'll explain everything; I promise." He widened his green eyes.

"But, what... how?" Liliana sputtered. She shivered, the water was getting colder.

The end of Ardus's tail twitched. "Since we've been together, have you ever been hungry or in danger? Have I ever led you wrong."

"No... I suppose not," Liliana admitted.

"All right then." The cat curled his tail. "You follow along, and things will be better than you ever imagined possible. Trust me."

"Fine." Liliana sulked, dropped the shoulders hunched around her ears. "But I hope you're right, because I'm freezing."

Ardus stood erect, cocking his head, listening to something only he could hear. "Don't worry, it's almost time."

"Time for what?" Liliana scanned the empty woods, mystified.

"Remember, you promised to follow along and trust me. You are now the Marquis of Carabas," Ardus told her before bounding away, leaving Liliana open mouthed in shock.

Although the trees blocked the road from Liliana's view, she heard a noise. A lot of noises. Horses, the rumble of carriages and voices mingled together, and above it all, Ardus's distinctive cat voice.

"Help! Help!" Ardus cried dramatically. Liliana couldn't see him, but she pictured him waving his little cat paws for his audience.

"Oh, its you." Liliana heard a vaguely familiar male voice. "What are you doing in Nanves?"

"My mistress," the cat cried, a tremble in his voice.

He really is a talented actor, thought Liliana, straining to listen.

"She stopped the carriage to go swimming and bandits attacked. They took everything. Everything. She only escaped by jumping into the river," Ardus raised his voice to a wail.

"Oh, we must help her. Guards."

"She's this way." Liliana heard the clatter of half a dozen men dismounting, crunching and crackling leaves and branches as Ardus led them to her swimming spot.

"Mistress, we're saved. These kind men have offered their assistance."

Liliana tried to look as dignified as possible. Which was not very dignified, considering she was half submerged in water. Liliana clutched her bathing cover to her chest, grateful for the Antarai custom of bathing modestly.

She waded to the edge of the water, taking the hand of a guard as he offered his help. Someone placed a warm blanket over her shoulders, for which Liliana was immensely grateful. It really was chilly.

"Is she all right?" Liliana heard a rustling in the trees and Prince Landry, accompanied by Prince Alex and Princess Celine, emerged. Trailing behind her was Prince Landry's mysterious companion, looking put out at the inconvenience.

"Oh, you poor thing. That must have been terrifying." Princess Celine rushed to Liliana's side. "Don't worry, you're safe now." Celine turned to her female companion, "Sophie, have you got the extra cloak? Would you be a dear and fetch it from the carriage?"

Sophie huffed, but didn't argue, turning to do Celine's bidding. Liliana was stunned into shy silence. Princess Celine, epitome of everything beautiful and brave, was here. In person. Speaking to Liliana, helping her.

"Oh dear, you can't walk to the carriage like this. You need shoes," Celine tutted over her purple toes. "Can someone get something for her feet, please?"

"No need," a deep voice answered. "I'll take care of it." She was swept up in a pair of muscular arms and held against a hard chest.

"Oh, I can walk," Liliana protested, before looking into a pair of mesmerising green eyes. Prince Landry smiled down at her, showing a dimple in his right cheek.

"We wouldn't want you to cut your feet on those sharp rocks." Landry tightened his grip.

Liliana relaxed; he was so warm. It wouldn't hurt to let him carry her to the carriage. After all, she couldn't argue with royalty.

Landry set Liliana down in Celine's carriage, where Sophie was waiting. Sophie smiled warmly at Prince Landry before giving Liliana a disdainful look.

"I don't really use the carriage much." Celine wrinkled her nose. "I like to ride where I can see everything. But Sophie or Louisa will get you something to wear. I think we're the same size." Celine gave Liliana an appraising look.

It was no easy feat in the confines of a carriage, but soon Liliana was dressed in a spare set of travelling clothes— soft breeches and a long tunic paired with supple leather boots. Sophie had sulkily produced the extra cloak which Liliana gratefully threw over the rest of the outfit. Leaving her damp hair down to dry, Liliana emerged.

A sea of curious faces eagerly waited for her, but Liliana's eyes rested on one familiar whiskered face. Ardus. He winked, nodding approvingly.

"I must say, it's a terrible thing that's happened to you. We insist you accompany us until you reach your accommodation." King Ruben, with Landry and Alex flanking either side, spoke.

"Thank you, Your Majesty." Liliana inclined her head in what she hoped was a regal way.

"We were headed toward the Marquis castle, in the Avre Mountains," Ardus spoke smoothly.

"What a coincidence." King Ruben smiled cheerily. "We're travelling that way ourselves. I insist you join us. That is, if you wish, of course." He paused, waiting for Liliana to respond.

"Um.." Out of the corner of her eye, Liliana saw Ardus nodding vigorously, green eyes gleaming. "Yes." Liliana stammered. "That would be lovely. Thank you so much." Still feeling shy in the presence of royalty, Liliana nervously twisted the ends of her damp hair.

"Excellent. It's settled." King Ruben beamed, striding back to his carriage, a large gilded affair.

Celine clapped her hands gleefully. "I'm so excited we'll have another girl with us," she crowed, shooting Landry and Alex a triumphant look. She took Alex by the arm, dragging him off in search for an appropriate mount. Liliana hoped it would be a calm one. Although her riding skills improved immensely in the past month, she didn't feel confident riding one of the King Ruben's high-spirited thoroughbreds.

Ardus spirited away on a mysterious cat errand as well, leaving Liliana alone with Landry. She breathed in the scent of bergamot and spice, which she associated with Landry's presence.

"So, you're the mysterious Marquis of Carabas." Landry slid Liliana a thoughtful look. "I must say, you had the castle in quite the uproar."

"I hope I didn't cause much trouble." Liliana gave him an anxious look.

"No, quite the opposite. Things were getting boring. I have to ask though... have we met before? You seem so familiar."

Liliana held her breath, hoping he didn't remember the time he had almost run her over with his horse in Annecy Market Square.

"I know." Landry snapped his fingers. "Liliana, we met In the hall. You must have sneaked in with your cat. You look different now."

"Yes, I was... undercover." Liliana glanced away, hoping desperately Ardus knew what he was doing. She hated lying.

"Well, your disguise worked. No one here has recognized you. Don't worry." Landry winked. "Your secret's safe with me. Your cat, on the other hand, is quite recognizable and memorable."

Liliana laughed, glad to move the topic onto safer ground. "Yes, Ardus is quite the character, isn't he?"

"However did you find him?"

"I think it's more like Ardus found me." Liliana relaxed. "He's the family cat, I guess you could say." She bravely glanced at Landry, her heart skipping a beat as their eyes met.

"We've found you a horse. Oh, am I interrupting?" an amused smile rested on Celine's lips as she looked back and forth between Liliana and Landry.

Liliana stepped hastily back, "We were just talking," she insisted, scolding herself. What was she thinking, lingering near Landry like this? Landry was the prince of Iasia and Liliana was just—just—Liliana didn't know exactly what she was at this particular moment, but she certainly shouldn't entertain fanciful ideas about princes. She followed Celine to a patient grey mare waiting for her.

"I thought you might ride with me." Celine handed the reins to Liliana. "Sophie came with us, but I don't think she actually likes horses. She'll stay in the carriage."

Liliana held out her hand, letting the mare get acquainted with her. "She's lovely. Thank you."

"Yes, well, you're actually doing me a favour. Sarah and Louisa like riding in the carriage with Sophie; it's always me and the stinky men riding." Celine wrinkled her nose, waving a hand at Alex, Landry and the guards. It'll be nice having another girl around. At least for a while.

Liliana swung into the saddle, grateful for the riding skills the Antarai taught her over the past few weeks. Arus appeared from wherever he had been lurking, jumping lightly in front of her.

"We'll stay in Nanves tonight and start riding into the mountains tomorrow. There are a lot of smaller villages up there, and Ruben wants me to greet them, so I can meet the people." Celine tossed her flowing golden hair as she guided her horse along the road.

Nanves was a ten-minute ride away, and soon the party found themselves ensconced in the best inn Nanves offered, a two story wooden affair covered with a riot of ivy and climbing flowers.

"Do you want to come to Market Square with Sophie and I?" Celine knocked on Liliana's door. "I hear there's a fabulous selection of venders."

"I'd love to." Liliana got up off the bed where she had been resting and soon she was strolling arm and arm down the main street with Celine and the reluctant Sophie, closely followed by Sarah and Louise, Celine's two ladies-in-waiting.

"Alex and Landry said they'd meet us here. Alex doesn't trust me in markets. I have a bit of a history of running into misadventure." Celine pushed back her golden mane of hair until it fell down her back like a waterfall.

"And then you have to meet the mayor and the town council," reminded Sarah.

"Oh, yes, that." Celine sighed. "We meet the mayor in every town." She turned to explain to Liliana, "He tells us what a wonderful place it is, what the trade is like etc. etc. I wouldn't mind, but it takes forever. Obviously, I love the people, so I'm glad to do it." She tacked on the last sentence hurriedly after receiving a reprimanding look from Sarah.

Liliana followed the girls into the square where throngs of well-wishers crowded them, piling flowers and gifts on Celine. After politely receiving them, Celine passed the gifts on to Sarah and Louise who were soon laden with a collection of items including several bunches of flowers, a painted china tea service in a fancy presentation box, and several lengths of fabric, which the girls oohed and ahhed over before returning them to their paper wrappings. Even Sophie forgot to sulk for a moment as she admired the fine wools and gossamer silks.

"Look, there're the boys." Celine waved vigorously at Landry and Alex, accompanied by a selection of guards. They were sipping a dark amber liquid out of tall, narrow glass mugs.

"What is that?" Celine wrinkled her nose at the foaming liquid.

"It's Nanves traditional cider." Landry took another slurp of the liquid. "Want to try some? They make it with forest apples."

Celine took a suspicious sip from Alex's mug. "Oh, that is good." Her face lit up with a surprised laugh. She nodded encouragingly at the girls; instantly mugs of cider were procured and passed to all.

Sophie took a cautious sip, pursing her lips and setting the cup aside, but the rest of the group enjoyed the hot spiced drink. A vendor handed them a plate of nutmeg cakes and the sweetness melted deliciously in Liliana's mouth.

Warmed by the hot drink, the group rambled across Market Square to the town hall where the mayor of Nanves, a rotund man with slicked back hair and a smooth voice, effusively greeted them.

Liliana hesitated outside the hall as Sophie pushed her aside with a huff, but Landry waved Liliana in, smiling encouragingly at her reticence. The mayor ushered them into a spacious room decorated with large murals depicting bygone battles. Carved columns were interspersed along the walls, and glass windows faced the looming mountains on one side.

After a long speech welcoming the royal party, the mayor concluded grandly, sitting down. That wasn't so bad, thought Liliana, until another man, dressed similarly to the mayor stood, giving a nearly identical and equally long speech. And so it went. When the last speech finished, pins and needles were crawling up Lilian's legs from sitting motionless for so long.

"Are the mayor's speeches this long in every town?" Liliana whispered to Landry.

He nodded. "Yes, part of the job. We get used to it. And we love seeing the country and meeting people. But they mostly want to show off their town. To learn what the local issues are, Alex and I will conduct some covert digging." Landry laughed at Liliana's questioning look. "I'll show you later," he promised, "but first dinner."

Liliana pushed her curiosity aside as the dinner in honour of the royal family was served in the town hall that night. All the important townspeople were present; Liliana noticed the mayor of Nanves sitting ostentatiously at the head of the table as townspeople scurried to make last-minute preparations. Lost without her Antarai friends and not sure of the protocol, Liliana stuck close to the girls, following their actions.

At last, the mayor led them to a long table covered with starched white linen. Soon, they were digging into bowls of steaming soup placed in front of them. Liliana relaxed a bit. Soup isn't too complicated, Liliana thought as she took a bite. Soon, Liliana was in the swing of things, and by the last course, fresh fruit served with slices of creamy cheese, she felt like a part of the close-knit group.

"Now, are you ready to learn what Nanves really thinks?" Landry whispered as they were ushered into carriages—absurd for the short distance to the inn, but who was Liliana to argue.

"I think so." Liliana felt a prickle of excitement, wondering what Landry and Alex were planning.

"Right, put these on; meet use at the stables in ten minutes." Landry passed Liliana a cloth wrapped parcel.

Liliana returned to her room, quickly unwrapping the parcel to discover it held a nondescript tunic and a tattered pair of breeches. Pulling on the breeches and the tunic, Liliana tied her hair loosely and hurried down the flight of wooden steps leading from the back of the inn to the stable yard.

"You'll do nicely, just add this." Joined by the two brothers, Celine appeared from behind a bale of hay and plunked a woven cap on Liliana's head. The cap slid down until it nearly covered her eyes.

"What is it we're doing?" Liliana tucked in her hair, adjusting the cap so she could see.

"Meeting people, of course. Real people." Celine grinned. She had tied back her golden curtain of hair and covered it with a floppy felt hat.

"We started this a while ago," Landry explained, noticing Liliana's perplexed expression. "Celine wore... a disguise for a time. She noticed what people said to her as Princess Celine was dramatically different from when she was passing as a regular citizen. So now we do this." He waved a hand, circling himself. Landry dressed as a farmer, wearing a pair of large muddy boots and a checked wool jacket. A large kerchief hanging from his back pocket completed the look.

"Meet Franz." Landry smiled.

"We want to learn what Iasian citizens truly think. This seemed the best idea," Alex explained, adjusting his threadbare cloak.

"Are you up for it?" Landry winked.

"Of course." Liliana wished she could explain she actually was a regular citizen, so there was no need to disguise herself as one. But this seemed a wonderful adventure.

"I'll accompany you as well. Obviously, disguised as a regular, common cat." Ardus stood, stretching and yawning from his curled up position on a pile of feed sacks.

"I'll carry you." Liliana unhooked a shawl hanging on a peg, wrapping the little cat until only his eyes and ears peeked out.

"We'll have to split up. There's too many of us." Celine pursed her lips thoughtfully. "I'll go with Alex and you go with Landry." She decided. "And no guards. I'll can take care of anything we come across." She smiled, resting her hand on the hilt of her sword, her only concession to the farmhand look she'd created.

Liliana glanced at Landry, who raised an eyebrow, challenging her. She raised her chin in response, stepping forward.

"All right, then. Let's go." Celine took Alex's arm and swung around, leaving Landry and Liliana standing alone.

Landry waited a few minutes before poking his head out of the stable door. The only person was a stable boy, busily polishing a saddle. Landry motioned for Liliana to follow, and they were off.

"So, I thought we could start at the tavern." Landry led Liliana down the narrow, cobbled street. "Celine and Alex are going to explore the market."

"Of course." Liliana gulped; the last time she'd been in a tavern, she'd been serving. She followed Landry to the square. The tavern, the Red Lion, was easily the busiest place in Nanves. The scent of roasted meat and fried onions drifted across the street to where Liliana and Landry stood. People spilled out the door, sitting at large wooden tables placed outside. Liliana followed Landry through the crush, finding a seat at one of the long wooden tables inside. The tavern was warm and loud; Landry had to shout for the barmaid to hear his order.

"Aren't you worried people will recognize you?" she whispered. The familiar slicked back hair of the mayor bobbed up and down as he gestured animatedly to his neighbour.

"You would think." Landry rolled his eyes. "But they see our position more than they see us. No one's noticed yet."

A barmaid set two bowls of spicy stew in front of them, accompanied by mugs of tangy cider that seemed the Nanves drink of choice.

"How do you get people speak to you?" Liliana blew on the hot stew.

"Easy. Watch." Landry cleared his throat.

"Terrible, what happened in the west, isn't it?" Landry addressed Liliana in a loud voice, including the farmer across the table with a friendly glance. The beefy farmer, sleeves rolled up to reveal brawny forearms, took the bait.

"Oh, aye." the man responded, eager to share what he knew with any listening ears. "I've never heard anything like it. I tell you, it was bad. Terrible."

Landry threw Liliana a subtle wink. "I heard it was bad. Did they send soldiers from the outpost?"

The man shook his head. "You know the army leaves magic alone, unless there's a royal decree. Colonel Glendo sent men to clean and repair though. It was good of him."

"All because of the girl?" Landry continued conversationally.

The man scoffed, "Girl? That was no girl. Wasn't what she seemed at all. Took everyone by surprise."

Liliana felt Ardus, who until now lay curled and relaxed against her chest, stiffen. He remained in his hiding place. Tense. Listening.

"Oh yes, that's right. And she was..." Landry let the words trail enticingly.

"A shapeshifter." The farmer took the bait, leaning forward and lowering his voice to a hoarse whisper. "Not just any shapeshifter. A shapeshifter that can assume limitless forms. Something more powerful than ever before." The farmer paused for maximum effect.

"People say she's really an ogre. An extremely potent ogre too by the looks of it." The farmer leaned back, large elbows on the table, slugging cider.

Liliana's breath caught in the back of her throat. This was the same ogre bothering the Antarai. It had to be. She wished briefly she was in the Antarai campsite, sitting around the safety of the fire. But she trusted Ardus; if this was how Liliana needed to help the Antarai, she would do her best.

"Where did the ogre came from?" Landry tried to keep his voice casual, but Liliana heard an underlying note of concern.

"That's the thing." The farmer removed his cap and scratched his head. "No one knows exactly where she came from. Some insist she had holed up in the mountains and only recently emerged. Others say she crossed the border from Lovan. You know, they're a suspicious lot. The ogre wouldn't have gathered enough power over there. Would have snuffed her right out. Not that I agree with that. But in this case.... Might not have been a terrible thing."

Others at the table began taking an interest in the conversation. Among them, the mayor who was fidgeting in his seat, looking uncomfortable, beads of sweat forming around his hairline. He sipped his drink, a rich red wine.

Liliana wondered what the source of the mayor's awkwardness was, and her question was soon answered as a roughly dressed man in a soiled leather jerkin tossed him a scornful look.

"If Nanves wasn't so busy getting ready for fancy visitors, we might have had more help." A sneer spread across his face.

The mayor squirmed in his seat, the pompous expression he'd sported earlier disappearing.

"It isn't every day we have royalty visiting," the mayor protested weakly.

"All I'm saying is instead of organizing a big dinner for your fancy pants guests, your efforts would have been better spent giving the ones whose homes were destroyed a roof over their heads." The farmer glared at the mayor over the scarred wooden table.

Liliana cringed, sneaking a glance at Landry, wondering how he felt about the slight, but Landry remained apparently unbothered. He casually spooned another bite of stew into his mouth, observing the interaction. His leg twitched under the table, but otherwise, he stayed quiet.

"It's the royal family," argued the mayor, oily hair shining. "We need them on our side. They're the only ones who can help."

The farmer snorted. "Not likely. You know they'll prance into town, flags flying, wave, then bog off like always."

The mayor tightened his lips. Clearly, this was a well-worn argument. "Well, what do you advise?"

By now, the conversation had drawn more attention. Heads were turning. Liliana wondered how long it would be before they blew their cover. Not that Liliana had to worry, she was already a commoner.

The mayor swirled his red wine, staring thoughtfully at the dark liquid. "We're going to have to fight. I just don't know how. I'll speak to King Ruben tomorrow." His head drooped.

The farmer, pacified by the mayor's conciliatory gesture, settled back in his seat and began eating again.

Not wanting to linger in the tavern, Liliana and Landry slipped out quickly after. By now it was dark, their path only lit by dim squares of light shining from the windows along street front. Liliana caught her foot on the rough edge of the cobblestone and stumbled.

"Oops, careful there." A warm hand caught her elbow. Liliana was suddenly very aware that they were alone in the dark. The fresh scent of bergamot surrounded her; Landry was so close, she could feel his warm breath stirring her hair. Heart racing, she took a step back, gathering her thoughts.

"I have to say, that was enlightening." Landry commented as they headed for the stables where they promised to meet Celine and Alex.

"Do Iasians always complain about the royal family?" Liliana stepped carefully over a loose cobblestone.

"Rarely, but if something goes wrong, they need someone to blame. It's easier to blame us, I guess. I mean, my brother has it the worst; he has to be king someday. I'm the spare; Alex and father take the brunt of the complaints." Landry opened the door to the stable, immersing them in the warm scent of hay, horses and leather.

Celine and Alex were back; Celine was lounging back against a hay bale cleaning her sword.

"Did you learn anything?" Alex asked eagerly.

"Apparently there's an ogre giving people trouble." Landry sat on a wooden bench, his eyes worried.

Liliana unwound the shawl from where Ardus had been hiding. He perched next to Landry, curling his tail delicately around his paws.

"We heard about the ogre too." Celine slid the polished sword back into the scabbard.

"Apparently, it's a shapeshifter." She exchanged a concerned glance with Alex.

"Should we warn father?" Landry asked Alex.

"No, father disapproves of us going without guards. Safety and all that. The mayor plans to tell him tomorrow."

"Have you heard about the ogre elsewhere?" Liliana wondered.

"No, this is the thing. Nanves is the first place we've heard of it. But the news is from several unique sources. It must be legitimate."

"If it's a shapeshifter, we're going to need magic. The army wouldn't be able to handle it on their own. Remember what happened with Cherry? We almost lost Celine when she shifted into her double." Alex's eyes bore a look of apprehension. "Have we got any mage's in the outpost?"

Landry shook his head. "No. We've never needed mages here before. It's mostly the Antarai in the mountains; they're powerful enough to tend to their own troubles."

Alex rubbed the back of his neck with his hand. "I'll send messages to Florin immediate to send mages. And we'll have to speak to father. It's just finding the best way to approach him."

"Well, it could be worse. We could have to tell mother." Landry grinned at his brother, trying to lighten the tone. However, the tightness around his eyes told Liliana of his concern.

"Do you think you should tell them to bring the sceptre?" Celine stood, brushing the straw from her clothes.

Landry and Alex exchanged worried glances.

"I can't send for the sceptre without father's approval." Alex hesitated, "I'll speak to him in the morning." He joined Celine, slipping into the darkness.

"Do you think a mage can defeat the ogre?" Liliana's eyes searched Landry's. Although the story of Celine's encounter with the shapeshifter hadn't been made public, whispers and rumours abounded with stories of the power and cunning of the ogre shapeshifter. It ended with the disappearance of one of the royal Lavonian council members under extremely mysterious circumstances; most people suspected the shapeshifter played a large part in the saga.

Landry scratched his chin thoughtfully. "I hope so. If they bring the sceptre, we'll have a chance. And with Alex, we can weed out any ill intentions. Alex is an emotive, you know."

"He is?" Liliana had heard of this strange gift of sensing other's feelings and intentions, but she had never met one. Not to her knowledge, anyway.

"Yes, Alex keeps quiet about it, but it comes in handy more often than not."

"And what about you? Do you have any special abilities?" The darkness gave Liliana the confidence to ask personal questions.

Landry laughed. "Who, me? Not that I know of. I'm the second son. Everything went to Alex first." Although his words were blunt, his tone was light-hearted.

"Are you two planning to flirt all evening, or will I get some sleep tonight?" Ardus eyed Landry, a grumpy expression on his furry face.

Through the dim light, Liliana caught a hint of red rising in Landry's cheekbones as he quickly stood and stretched.

"That cat of yours is right." Landry put a hand over his mouth, yawning. "It's late and we've got a busy morning."

Liliana scooped Ardus in her arms and together they walked back to the inn.

"ARE YOU SURE THE ANTARAI don't mind me going without them?" Liliana was in her room the next morning, lacing herself into a dress. The tour was continuing on to the next town, and Landry and the royal party had convinced Liliana to accompany them.

"No, the Antarai don't mind. We stick to the plan," Ardus's voice was huffy. "This is what they wanted all along. Now, if you're ready, I'm starving. That stable was picked clean by barn cats and I need breakfast." He paced up and down the bed, watching Liliana fumble with the intricacies of her dress.

"Why are you wearing that dress anyway? Isn't it a bit.... fancy for traveling?" Ardus eyed the rich fabric distastefully. Celine had sent Liliana a selection of clothes, and the color had drawn her to this one, a rich emerald green that shimmered under the light.

"Do you think it's too much?" Liliana looked in the mirror, hesitantly fingering the embroidered neckline.

Ardus cocked his head to the side. "Maybe a little. It's like you're trying to impress someone... wait a minute. It's him, isn't it?" the little cat's green eyes gleamed. "I knew it!" he cried triumphantly.

Liliana ripped off the dress, fighting the blush staining her cheeks. "No, that's not it at all," she protested, choosing a dark brown travelling gown and stuffing herself into it. "I just wanted to fit in. I'm a regular person, and I'm in over my head here." She turned pleading eyes to Ardus.

"Oh, I see." If cats could smirk, Ardus would be smirking. He sat bolt upright, neatly cleaning his whiskers with dainty grey paws. "So the fancy dress has absolutely nothing to do with the handsome, young... er... did I say handsome?"

"No." Liliana threw the green dress at Ardus, who nimbly darted out of its path.

"Just remember. Prince Landry might be Iasian royal family now, but a few years ago, he wasn't a prince. He was the mere son of a duke and duchess. Not even an important duke and duchess. They got their position by default. Just like you got yours."

"What do you mean, just like I got mine? I don't have a title." Liliana sat at the mirror and began brushing her hair, stroking the long dark locks until they shone.

"Of course you do. You're the Marquis of Carabas," Ardus huffed.

"But I'm not the Marquis of Carabas," Liliana argued.

"Of course, you are." The little cat twitched his tail irritably.

Liliana huffed in displeasure. She could get nowhere with that creature. Finally, content with her hair, she picked up the little cat in her arms, annoyance fading as she stroked the soft fur and headed down to breakfast.

The mountains were immense. Liliana didn't realize how immense until later that day. They left Nanves behind and proceeded straight toward the looming heights. Although the weather here was warm, snow covered the tops of the ancient peaks year-round, jagged teeth laced with icy white crystal.

"Beautiful, aren't they?" Landry rode up next to Liliana.

"Magnificent, I could look at them forever," Liliana admitted.

"We lived in our mountain estate part of every year until we moved to Florin," Landry told her. "I loved it. The cold air so fresh. So much freedom." A pensive expression flitted through the green eyes.

"Do you miss them?" Liliana asked.

Landry thought for a moment. "I do. I try not to think about it. There's no point. Life's changed so much now." He smiled at her. "By the way, where's that sarcastic cat of yours. I have heard none of his cheeky comments yet today."

Liliana laughed. "Ardus went on ahead. Said he wanted a peace and quiet."

They were approaching a vast orchard. The fruit was only ripening, boughs nodding under the heavy fruit. Apples, pears, and even plums, rich purple peeking through glossy green leaves.

"That's a lovely orchard," commented Landry as they passed through a grand iron gate. The road wound through the centre of the orchard. Trees spreading all directions as far as Liliana could see. Soon, the sound of birds surrounded them as the sweet-scented breeze rustled through the leaves.

In the distance, Liliana watched a group of farmers accompanied by the orchardist, a rangy man wearing a long overcoat and wide brimmed felt hat; his status was clear by the animated instructions he was giving his workers. Soon, the workers scattered through the trees.

"Hello," Landry called to the orchardist, waving from his horse.

"Your Highness." The orchardist tipped his hat respectfully.

"This is a fine orchard you have," King Ruben poked his head from the carriage to speak to the orchardist.

"Thank you, Your Majesty. We work very hard here. If the weather holds, we'll have an excellent crop," the orchardist replied. The brim of the hat shaded his eyes from the bright sun, preventing Liliana and Landry from seeing his face.

By now, others had gathered. King Ruben climbed out of his carriage to join the conversation.

"We were also admiring this man's orchard," Landry remarked to King Ruben.

King Ruben glanced around, his brow furrowed. "It is a very nice orchard. I don't actually remember passing through here before. Who does it belong to? Is there an estate nearby?"

The orchardist smiled. "This orchard actually belongs to the Marquis of Carabas."

Liliana bit her tongue; her heart thumping against her ribcage.

"Is that so?" Liliana squirmed as King Ruben slid her a speculative look.

"Oh yes. These orchards have been in the Carabas family for generations."

"Well, I need to stretch my legs. We must take a walk and enjoy these impressive surroundings. Maybe you could give us a tour." King Ruben looked at Liliana, a broad smile crossing his face.

"Of course, Your Majesty." Liliana gulped. Handing the reins to a guard, she dismounted. With the two princes, Celine, Sophie and King Ruben fanning out behind her, she waded through the tall grass surrounding the trees.

"Ahem. As you can see, these orchards contain several types of fruit. The apple, the pear, and..." Liliana squinted at one of the low hanging purple fruits. "The plum." She paused, hoping desperately no one would ask troublesome questions.

"I see. Very interesting mixing them like this. Is there a reason behind that?"

"Oh, yes." Liliana nodded wisely as she inwardly cursed the blasted cat for putting her into this situation. "But perhaps the orchardist would be best at explaining the reasoning behind it." She gave the orchardist a hopeful smile.

"It helps with the harvest, Your Majesty. If we have different fruits, people can work the orchards year-round. Besides the trees, we have a cider making facility as well. Perhaps you're familiar with the cider in these parts. It contains the mixture from this orchard."

"Is that where the cider comes from?" Landry perked up; he was fond of the local cider, even sending barrels back to Florin. "Why didn't you tell us, Liliana? You're so modest." He threw Liliana a teasing look. Sophie scowled, tossing her head and taking Landry possessively by the arm.

"Yes. Your highness. I only run the orchard, the cider master runs the mill..."

"We must have a tour of the cider mill," King Ruben declared. "That cider is fantastic, I don't know why it's not being exported." He shot Liliana a pointed look.

"Um... I guess I never really thought about it," Liliana replied awkwardly. "I suppose we could look into exporting."

The orchardist pointed down a small one lane track leading to the cider mill, and the party set off. The mill was huge, a group of large stone structures, topped with a timber roofs and sides. Liliana peeked into a set of double doors as they went by and saw rows of large wooden caskets lined up neatly in the dim interior. This was quite the operation.

The cider master had gotten wind of their arrival and came to meet them, wiping wrinkled hands on a large cloth tied around his waist.

"Welcome, Your Majesty, your Highness." He bowed low.

"We heard this is where you make that delicious cider." Landry lost no time getting to the point.

"Yes, we make quite a lot of cider here." The cider master beckoned them inside. The bustle of activity awed Liliana. Large draft horses strained against their harnesses as they pulled the massive cider presses, and the sweet apple scent was thick in the air. What was Ardus thinking, telling everyone she owned this?

The cider master ushered them to a long wooden table, pouring foamy mugs of cider out of a large glass jug for them to sample.

"So refreshing." Celine sipped elegantly, hands dwarfed by her huge mug. "You should have told us about your mill; we could have travelled here first."

"I didn't think you would be interested." Liliana stalled for time, muttering inward threats toward Ardus. What else was the cat keeping from her; and what would happen when they found out she wasn't the Marquis of Carabas? She shivered in spite of the warmth of the cider mill.

Finally, they were done. Liliana managed to bluff her way through the tour, letting the cider master do most of the talking, before they returned to the carriages. Since the orchard and the cider press village only comprised a small collection of houses, they moved on. Tonight, they would be in camp.

Royal camping was remarkably different from the casual yet streamlined campsites of the Antarai people. King Ruben liked to travel in comfort and style. Several luxuriously furnished tents were provided for the royal family, and Liliana was soon ensconced in her own tent. Liliana's tent was enormous, with enough space to stand and walk around. They placed a bed complete with a feather comforter and an array of cushions in the corner, with a cluster of seats set around a brass brazier. They even covered the floor with a patterned rug. Liliana sat on a cushioned seat, biting into a spiced raisin tart. She might as well eat while she had the opportunity. The tart stuck in her throat as if it were sawdust. She dreaded King Ruben's reaction when the real Marquis of Carabas showed up. That dratted cat.

"Here you are. Did they bring anything for me?" Ardus pranced through the tent flap, swinging his tail behind him. Ignoring Liliana's glare, he hopped in her lap, rubbing his head against her hand, asking for a scratch under his chin.

Liliana clenched her fist. This was a step too far. "How dare you?" she hissed. "King Ruben thinks I own all those orchards. What are they going to do when they learn I'm a fraud?" Angry tears pricked the back of her eyes.

"I wouldn't worry about that." The cat examined the table, turning his nose up at the raisin tarts. "Did they even bring milk for the tea?" Ardus pointedly eyed the small jug on the table. Liliana huffed, pouring milk into her saucer, and placed it at the edge of the table.

"Thank you. I have to tell you, it was thirsty work today." The cat lapped at the milk, cleaning his whiskers fastidiously when the saucer was empty before kneading Liliana's lap and curling up comfortably.

"Now, listen to me," Liliana protested. "This has to stop. You can't go around telling everyone I'm the Marquis of Carabas—whoever that is—you're going to get me in trouble when they find out I'm not the Marquis," Liliana's voice rose.

"They won't." Ardus closed his eyes sleepily, basking in the heat of the brazier.

"What do you mean they won't find out I'm not the Marquis of Carabas? Of course, they will. Those orchards and the cider mill clearly belonged to someone. I can't take all the credit."

"Of course, they do. They belong to the Marquis. No one was lying about that."

"Did anyone ever tell you you're infuriating?" Liliana gave in and rubbed the soft grey fur under Ardus's chin.

"Frequently," Came the sleepy reply. "Just for a little while longer. I promise everything will be fine."

A few hours later, Liliana peeked into what she assumed was the dining tent.

"Over here." Celine waved Liliana over to her. Liliana, lured out of her tent by the smell of roasted meat, had followed her nose into the tent. Cunning tables were folded out and Celine, Sophie, and the prince brothers were nibbling from an array of platters.

"We're being casual; you can help yourself," Celine advised, forking tender roast pork onto her plate.

Liliana timidly placed a small selection on her plate and began eating. The food was delicious.

"We bring one of father's cooks with us. He never stops complaining about the lack of kitchen facilities, but he's well worth the earful if you ask me," Landry whispered in Liliana's ear. His breath tickled the side of her face, causing butterflies to run riot in Liliana's stomach. She lowered her eyes under Sophie's glare.

"We'll reach Antarai territory tomorrow." Alex took a sip from his mug of cider.

"Oh, I've always wanted to meet the Antarai. I hear their embroidery is out of this world. I hope King Ruben lets us visit a marketplace and shop."

The two brothers exchanged wary glances. "Maybe with guards." Alex said reluctantly.

"Why, is it dangerous?" a determined glint shone in Celine's eyes as her hand automatically fingered her sword.

"Antarai are dangerous." Sophie narrowed her eyes.

"Antarai are unpredictable." Landry shot Liliana a cautious look, and a shiver ran down her spine. She wondered if Landry remembered her Antarai finery from their meeting in Florin.

"Liliana, you're from these mountains, what do you think of the Antarai?" Celine's blue eyes questioned.

"The Antarai are the most lovely, loyal people I ever met," Liliana spoke honestly.

Celine shot the brothers a triumphant look. "See. Nothing to worry about."

"It's up to Father, obviously," Alex spoke tactfully, knowing better than to argue with his impulsive wife when she became fixated on something.

The next morning they did not leave early. First, they had breakfast. A long, drawn-out affair. Liliana had noticed the grumbling chef earlier stirring a large pot over the fire and mumbling about too much smoke. But again, the food was delicious. Smooth porridge with honey, an array of cheeses and meats and even sliced fruit.

"He stocks up in every town," Landry explained to Liliana as she gazed at the giant platters of food in amazement. They all ate together in the large dining tent, the guards laughing and chatting among themselves and even Sarah and Louise forgetting their shyness and joining in the banter.

When breakfast finished, the party leisurely took down the tents and packed their belongings. Liliana felt lost in the confusion. So when Celine opted to have a practice session—insisting she didn't want to get rusty—Liliana opted to follow, settling on a dry log to watch.

Celine was good. Really good. Leaping and darting through the air, the sword a mere blur in her hand. Liliana wondered at the dedication it must take to gain such skill.

"She's pretty amazing, isn't she?" Landry found Liliana and plunked himself down next to her, crossing his long legs in front of him.

"Fantastic," Liliana admitted, peeking into his deep green eyes.

"Perfect for my brother. He needed some of fire in his life." Landry's eyes crinkled as he smiled. Liliana's heart gave a little skip in response.

"Where's that little cat of yours?" Landry scanned the area as if Ardus might appear at any minute. The fact was that Ardus had left early that morning. Although not before strongly hinting a request for fish from the cook would be highly appreciated. Then Ardus slipped off like a tiny shadow, melting into the trees.

After Celine finished her practice session, they were finally ready to go. The sun was high, but a mountain breeze protected them from the heat. The orchards were miles in the distance; they were climbing the lower foothills. In spite of the rugged hills, the soil was rich, even richer than the farmland Liliana called home. A variety of crops grew in the foothills; rows of green stretched across the mountain folds.

"Marvellous," King Ruben exclaimed, when stopped to water and rest the horses. "Just wonderful. Look at all of this farmland. I'm surprised I don't remember it from the last tour." The king examined his surroundings, taking it all in.

On one hillside field, farmers were busily moving up and down the rows, harvesting a kind of root vegetable. Large woven baskets held piles of roots, and in the distance, Liliana spotted baskets being loaded into a wagon for market.

King Ruben took a walk to see more.

"Hello there. That's a lovely crop you've got this year," the king greeted one of the farmers, who tipped back his wide brimmed straw hat in response.

King Ruben leaned down to examine the plants, ignoring his cloak dragging on the muddy ground.

"We had a lot of farmland on our estate before we moved to Florin," Landry explained as they watched King Ruben join in an animated discussion with the farmer. "He's always loved the land. I think that's why he came on the tour. He's interested in Iasian agriculture. Wants to expand trade."

King Ruben was gesturing at Liliana, beckoning her to join the conversation. Liliana felt a dart of apprehension as she saw King Ruben's smiling face. Somehow, she suspected it involved Ardus.

"Young Lady, you didn't tell me this was your farmland," scolded King Ruben.

Liliana gulped. "Oh, didn't I? I'm sorry, Your Majesty." She dipped her head politely, hiding her confusion.

"This young man told me all farmland west of that river belongs to Marquis of Carabas."

"Um—yes? I mean, yes. Yes, it does," Liliana agreed quickly. "We are quite lucky to have such lovely farmland." She smiled politely at the farmer, who winked. "We've been growing lots of...."

"Carrots, beets, and this year we're starting walnut trees. They keep the topsoil fertile," the farmer supplied helpfully. He pointed at the tidy rows of trees interspersed among the other plants.

"Absolutely," Liliana agreed. To be honest, with her father being in trade, she didn't have any experience farming other than her vegetable garden; she desperately hoped they wouldn't ask difficult questions.

"Well. I should let you get return to your vegetable field." Laughed King Ruben. Ignoring the dust and dirt, he shook the farmer's hand vigorously before returning to the party. "You are quite full of surprises." King Ruben gave Liliana a speculative look, a look that sent prickles of disquiet down her spine. She didn't know how much longer she could keep this charade up.

Liliana nodded weakly, returning to her horse.

"We're about a mile or two away from a small village explained Landry. We're going to do a walkthrough and greet everyone."

Liliana hid her worries behind a smile, hoping that this village didn't belong to the Marquis.

CHAPTER 18

As Liliana remounted her pony, she spotted smoke. Thick black smoke trickling, then pouring heavy, staining the clear blue sky an oily black.

Then she smelled smoke. A burning, choking smell clogging her throat. Luciana coughed and spluttered as it crept through the trees.

"The village is on fire!" Alex called. He reined in his horse, who fidgeted at the smoke, attempting to bolt down the mountain.

The guards instantly sprung into action, ushering King Ruben into his carriage and surrounding it, weapons drawn.

"Should we investigate?" Celine's hand crept toward her sword.

"No," King Ruben spoke, leaning through the carriage window. "You and Alex stay where it's safe. The guards will investigate the fire."

"I'll go," Landry volunteered. Sophie stepped forward, torn between avoidance of danger and desire to be with Landry.

"I will too," Liliana spoke, surprising g even herself. But she needed to help. The ogre could attack innocent villagers in the heat of the fire. Homes and livelihoods destroyed. The knowledge tore at her heartstrings. Liliana determined she would help any way possible.

"Are you sure, Liliana?" Landry crinkled his brow in concern.

"I'm certain," Liliana nodded, lips pressed together.

"Here, take my sword." Celine unbuckled her sword, handing the weapon to Liliana.

Armed with a sword she couldn't wield, Liliana, Landry and two guards rode toward the village. The smoke rose thick and bitter as they approached the village. Eyes watering, Liliana squinted through the haze. The horses were so nervous that it took all of Liliana's concentration to control her mount. She almost didn't notice the little girl. Running out of the trees, the child stumbled into the path, barefoot and sooty. Tears tracked through grey powder on her cheeks, turning into black trails.

Liliana scrambled from her horse. Dropping to a kneeling position beside the sobbing girl; Liliana gathered the child into her arms, murmuring soothing words into her ear.

"What happened?" she asked the girl who hiccupped, rubbing snot and tears into Liliana's shoulder.

"A scary monster," the girl sniffed, voice breaking. "He crashed things and made fires."

Liliana and Landry exchanged worried glances. The ogre?

"Can you tell me what the scary monster looked like? Maybe we could help." Liliana stroked the girl's sooty tangles.

The girl sniffed, tears dripping down her cheeks. "Enormous. As big as my cottage. And strong."

"Was the monster human or animal?" Landry asked the little girl, his voice gentle.

"Human. But ugly."

Liliana settled the little girl, leaving her with the guard who plied her with sweets stashed in his pocket.

"Do you think it's the ogre?" Liliana asked Landry in a low voice, glancing over her shoulder to check the child was out of earshot.

"The ogre is most likely," Landry whispered. "I'll continue on foot to investigate."

"I'll come too." Liliana decided.

The little girl calmed; the sweets had disappeared, but the guard had sat her on his knee, telling her a story. Liliana and Landry set off. Bending low and keeping silent, they followed the smoke through the trees.

Liliana was unprepared for the level of devastation the creature wreaked on the unsuspecting village. Modest cottages reduced to jagged heaps of smoking timber. Here and there, flames still broke out. Damaged fireplaces, Liliana thought, running appraising eyes over the village. People wandered the single street, lost expressions haunting their eyes. Injured villagers wandered among the chaos, some searching for missing family members. The village center; including the town hall and the market square were the epicentre of the attack. The Town Hall was a pile of crumbled stone scattered across the courtyard. The creature had decimated the market square, remnants of fruit and vegetables smashed and smeared through thick grit and rubble.

Tears sprang to Liliana's eyes as she surveyed the destruction. A warm hand circled her own; she looked down. Landry rubbed his thumb across the top of Liliana's, comforting her. At least the creature had left, disappeared into the mountains. Liliana shivered, wondering if the creature planned to return or if it intended to leave a swath of devastation as it travelled across the mountain villages.

"We need to learn more about this creature's intentions, but first let's help the villagers." She glanced at Landry, who set his jaw in determination. Striding to the centre of the town's former market square, Landry raised a commanding hand in the air. A few people looked up, vague interest crossing their faces at the richly dressed strangers appearing among them.

"Wait, isn't that the royal crest?" one woman asked, pointing. She adjusted a red kerchief over her hair, now grey from smoke and grit. Her comment drew attention. Soon, a small crowd clustered around Landry and Liliana.

"Brave people," Landry raised his voice so everyone could hear him speak. "The creature has wrought great evil today," a murmur of agreement went round as more villagers gathered.

"To overcome, all your strength, all your ingenuity, and all your fortitude is needed." Here, Liliana laid a gentle hand on Landry's arm to stop him. Standing on her tiptoes, she whispered into his ear. "Make the speech later. First douse the fires."

Liliana hoped she hadn't overstepped her bounds, but the village desperately needed practical help and someone to organize. Landry's eyes searched hers for a moment before he nodded.

"All right, what should we do first?"

"First find buckets, pour water over the fires. Organise a line with buckets from the water source."

Landry stepped onto a large rock, repeating Liliana's instructions. Eager for decisive action, buckets appeared, carried by eager villagers. The villagers formed a brigade from themarket square well. Another brigade formed from the brook running across the edge of the village. Soon, buckets of water were being passed hand to hand, soaking any remaining flames.

Next, Liliana sent for the village healer and injured people to be assessed in the market . One man broke his leg fighting when the ogre flung him into the side of a building. The creature had trapped a young boy in a barn that collapsed; his injuries weren't as severe as first appeared. The healer soon had him bandaged and resting quietly. The healer treated several minor injuries as well.

"They'll need food and shelter until they rebuild." Liliana had people salvage what they could from market, then had Landry find the village headman to ask about extra food stores.

By now King Ruben's guards had arrived in the village. They reunited the little girl with her relieved mother, who peppered her with grateful kisses.

"Are the rest of the party coming?" Liliana asked one of King Ruben's guards. "And have you got pen and parchment?"

"Why do you need pen and parchment?" Landry wondered as he brought the requested items.

"I want to write a note and send it to my farmers." Liliana sat with the pen. Grateful that her father had insisted she get an education, she began writing. "I'm getting food for the village." Liliana pressed her lips together, signing the note with a flourish before folding it into a heat square.

"Here," she handed the note to King Ruben's guard. "Can you find the wagon driver and pass him this message?"

The guard bowed his head, tucking the note away safely before riding away in a clatter of hoofbeats.

"Sit down and rest. You'll wear yourself out at that pace." Landry shoved a cup of water into Liliana's hands.

"Too much to do," Liliana complained, wiping her forehead with her sleeve, inadvertently leaving streaks of soot across her face. However, she accepted the water, thankful for the cool liquid that soothed her dry throat.

By evening, they had made significant progress. The royal party arrived, and their tents, along with the shelter salvaged from the wreck of the village, combined to create enough dry beds for everyone.

Not one but three wagons stuffed with food arrived from the Carabas farm, providing enough food to last until the villagers could sustain themselves again. The thought lurked at the edge of Liliana's mind; the actual Marquis of Carabas would eventually appear. What would he say about her stealing his identity? But she pressed on, pushing the fear aside; she'd worry about that later. People needed help.

King Ruben's chef was in his element. Soon, several large cooking fires crackled in Market Square, each with a large pot bubbling over it. Several women stepped up, volunteering to help cook. Chef Milot kept them busy, chopping and stirring and mixing.

The earthen oven in Market Square's center sustained minimal damage, and several men, under the strict eye of the baker, set to work repairing it. Soon, the smell of baking bread filled the town centre, causing mouths to water and spirits to lift.

Every bone and muscle ached as Liliana sat at the dinner table. Cobbled together with leftover wood from remains of market stalls, the table was one of many set up in Market Square. The steam from Liliana's vegetable soup wafted into her nostrils. Her stomach groaned at the rich, salty scent.

"Mind if we join you?" Celine and Sophie, followed by Alex and Landry, sat down next to Liliana.

"That was some fast thinking you did in the village today." Celine spooned soup into her mouth, closing her eyes at the velvety flavour.

"It was nothing," protested Liliana, blushing at the attention. "I did what anyone else would have done."

"You're too modest." Landry shot Liliana a proud look. "I saw you pitching in—helping—giving. Without you, this could've been a lot worse for everyone."

Sophie scowled, grumbling. "Of course, it's in Liliana's best interest. This is her land, after all." She picked at her bread with manicured fingers. She hadn't gotten near a speck of dirt all day.

"Well, I hope the village gets back on its feet before winter." Feeling uncomfortable with the scrutiny, Liliana deflected the attention.

"Most nobility doesn't care about their people nearly as much as you do, Liliana," Alex insisted. "As long as their estates are profitable, the people are immaterial."

Liliana squirmed. She wished more than ever that they knew the truth. She wasn't one of the nobility. Not even a little. And she certainly didn't deserve this effusive admiration.

Much to Liliana's relief, King Ruben strode over, cloak smudged with soot and hair streaked with ash and powder, but that didn't diminish his cheerful demeanor or his air of royalty.

"Ahem," clearing his throat, King Ruben called for attention.

"People of Trefle-Colline. Today, you met with tragedy. However, let's take a moment, to thank Liliana, Marquis of Carabas. She has stepped in and made survival possible today." King Ruben motioned for Liliana to stand.

Legs trembling, Liliana stood, twisting her hands at the many pairs of eyes turning her way. The crowd cheered and clapped, and Liliana overcame her shyness to dip her head in acknowledgement.

"Well done," Landry whispered; he reached over, squeezing Liliana's hand as people turned their attention back to their food. At least, Liliana thought, everyone was fed and sheltered. If for no other reason, the charade was worth it.

"Excuse me." a timid voice interrupted.

Liliana looked up, butter knife paused midair over her bread. A dirty-faced boy stood hesitantly at her elbow. About ten years old, he wore a course woven cap and clutching a coarse burlap pouch tight to his chest.

"Hello." Taken by his huge hazel eyes and toothy smile, Liliana scooted over, making room for the boy.

"Here." The little boy shoved the pouch in her direction. "For you."

Curious, Liliana took the pouch. Something soft and warm was moving inside. She opened the drawstring and a little furry head popped out.

"A kitten." Celine leaned forward, examining the kitten and reached out a finger to stroke the animal's soft grey fur. Blue eyes peered up as the kitten meowed, showing a pink mouth.

"For you," the little boy told Liliana, his voice serious.

"Why thank you, what a lovely gift. The most beautiful gift I've received." Liliana's heart warmed. Judging by his shy smile, the kitten was this little boy's most precious possession.

The little boy smiled.

"I have a secret." Liliana leaned close, lowering her voice. "I have a cat who is extremely jealous. I'm afraid that if I take the kitten *with* me, he might scratch him. So I need someone to take care of the kitten for me. Do you know anyone who loves cats?"

The little boy scratched his head. "Well, I suppose I'm already used to looking after Smoky. Maybe I could take care of him for you?"

Liliana tilted her head to one side, lips pursed. "Well, that might work. Would you be willing to do that? I'd pay you, of course."

The boy's eyes shone. "I'd take great care of the kitten," he vowed.

"I know you will." Liliana stroked the tiny kitten, admiring the softness of the fur before handing him back to his owner. Taking the last coins out of her small purse she carried, Liliana handed them to the little boy who tucked them into his pocket.

"Now, why don't we find milk for Smoky to drink," Liliana suggested. They found a bowl of milk and scraps of meat for the kitten, who lapped eagerly, covering its tiny whiskers with milky droplets.

"You are quite a brave boy to bring a kitten through the fires." Captivated by the little boy, Celine leaned forward to speak.

"Oh, yes." The little boy widened his hazel eyes. "I've never been so scared in all my life."

"Did you see the ogre? Can you tell us what it looked like?" Alex asked, keeping his voice gentle.

Liliana listened, leaning close to hear every word. In the bustle and effort, she hadn't opportunity to learn the details of what transpired.

The little boy perked up at the attentive audience, a proud expression crossing the thin face.

"It was a regular day. Most villagers travelled to Big Farm, but some were working our own gardens in the village. The creature appeared out of nowhere. Stomping around. It was really angry and really loud." He shivered.

"How big was creature?" Alex asked.

The little boy squinted in concentration. "Do you see that cottage?" he pointed to a two story thatched cottage across the square. "About that height. With wild hair. Long and tangly, like my sister when she gets out of bed in the morning. The creature's face was human, but hairy and ugly with giant tusks and a pig nose." The boy nibbled a slice of bread.

"And could the creature speak?" Alex prodded, "What did it say?"

"Well, it roared so loud, I was too scared to pay attention. Then I ran and hid under our stairs; that's how I didn't get hurt when the ogre smashed our cottage. I just held the kitten like this to keep him safe." His hazel eyes opened wide as he demonstrated, curling the small cat against his narrow chest.

"You did a wonderful job keeping him safe." The little boy glowed under the praise as all joined, admiring the little boy's bravery and cleverness.

The little boy was the first of many to thank Liliana for her decisive action. Soon, Liliana had a pile of gifts sitting at the table, including a vast pumpkin, a handful of beets, five shiny green stones, and a length of wool woven in a beautiful herringbone pattern.

"I can't believe they're so generous." Liliana fingered the wool, rolling the fibres between her fingers.

"They're grateful," Landry told her. "You did more than you know."

The padding of tiny feet and a furry body interrupted them as Ardus jumped onto Liliana's wool, rubbing against the fabric.

"Where have you been all day?" Liliana stroked Ardus furry head. A loud purr rumbled in his throat as he rubbed his head against Liliana's hand.

"Oh, looking around. Business," the little cat replied, his voice vague. Avoiding questions, he curled up on the wool, allowing Liliana to scratch under his chin. "Ow." He sat up as her hand caught something. A burr buried in his coat.

"How did you get burrs?" Liliana gently plucked Ardus's fur until the burr was loose enough to pull out. It wasn't like the fastidious Ardus to get things trapped in his glorious coat.

"In the woods. I ran into some underbrush," the cat replied mysteriously.

Liliana found three other burrs that she removed as Ardus murmured complaints. Finishing with a pat, she procured him a dish of food, which he devoured hungrily before falling asleep on her knee.

"He's quite the character, isn't he?" Landry watched the little cat as his paw twitched—an interesting dream, no doubt.

"You can say that again." Liliana lifted the tiny animal, who was so exhausted he didn't stir as she snuggled him under the blanket. Since they were providing shelter for the people of Trefle-Colline, she was sharing a tent with Celine, Sophie, Sarah and Louise. She curled beside the cat, letting her sore muscles relax into sleep.

CHAPTER 19

A loud noise woke Liliana. Her eyes snapped open, heart thudding in her chest.

Out of the pitch black darkness shrieked an inhuman roar so loud that it vibrated the flimsy tent with its intensity. Liliana's eyes snapped open, and she froze, ears cocked for any more sounds. There, out of the silence, emerged another roar. Closer than the last.

"Did you hear that?" Celine's voice was hoarse whisper.

Liliana nodded, before realizing Celine couldn't see the gesture in pitch black. "Yes." Liliana whispered, cringing at the suddenness of her voice, hoping the ogre had poor hearing. "Has the ogre returned?"

"I don't know." Celine answered. "But I'm going to prepare." Liliana heard a quiet rustling, then metal clinking. She assumed Celine was strapping on her sword.

"Are you sure that's a good idea?" she whispered. "I think it might be too big for us to fight outright."

"Well, I can't sit idle; I have to do *something*," Celine whispered. There was a swish and squeak of leather against leather as Celine pulled on her boots.

"I'll come too." Liliana surprised herself. She couldn't let Celine face the ogre alone. Liliana fumbled through the dark, pulling on her close with clumsy hands. Feeling around, she noticed Ardus's spot on the bed had grown cold. She bit her lip, hoping the cat was safe and out of harm's way. Throwing her cloak over her shoulder, she grabbed her dagger and followed Celine into the square.

The clouds obscured the moon and stars; Liliana felt her way through the square, guided only by the sound of Celine breathing. They didn't dare make light—that would put them in danger of attracting the attention of whatever creature lurked in the forest.

All around them, Liliana sensed quiet stirring as the entire village held their breath, waiting to see if the creature was back to wreak more destruction.

Liliana smelled bergamot and felt a familiar presence by her side. Landry. A warm hand took her cold one in his.

"You shouldn't be out here." Liliana felt Landry's breath in her hair as he leaned in close to whisper.

"I need to see what's happening." Liliana shivered as the creature roared again. It sounded like the creature was almost on top of them. Together, they shuffled through thick darkness, heading steadily toward the source of the roar.

They must have reached the edge of the village now, thought Liliana. The ground was rougher; Liliana stumbled over a rock. A strange smell filled the air, pungent. Rotten. A break in the clouds revealed a sliver of moonlight.

Liliana saw the creature, so close they could touch it. Liliana craned her neck. The ogre was tall, taller than the little boy's description. The ogre snorted; Liliana glimpsed cold, inhuman eyes—too small for the piglike face. They glittered through the trickling light. Horror washed over Liliana; every fibre of her being fought to run, but she stayed. Liliana locked every muscle into place, hoping the creature wouldn't find her.

The stench washed over her like a fog; Liliana struggled not to choke on the thick putrid smell. The creature froze, its head weaving side to side, searching for something, Liliana realized as an icy hand ran down her spine. Liliana's heart beat so fast she could hear the blood rushing through her veins. The creature sniffed the air, snorting through its pig nose.

Curiously, the creature wore fine fabric, although the clothing was clumsy, sewn with large awkward stitches. A large swath of velvet draped across its chest and over its head in a long cloak-like dress that drifted in the chilly wind. This mystified Liliana; she'd seen pictures of ogre's, and never had come across one dressed so... human before.

After pausing, the creature moved on, crashing through the trees and heading further west, toward the higher mountains.

After a few minutes, Liliana could breathe again. She moved, rolling her shoulders, but Landry stilled her with his hand.

"Wait," he whispered. "It might circle back."

Liliana's legs were stiff by the time Landry deemed it safe to move again, and her teeth chattered from cold. They returned to their tents, creeping through the darkness, not wanting to alert the ogre to their presence. It would be disastrous to draw the ogre back to the village.

"What do you think the ogre wanted?" Liliana asked. The creature had been searching for something in its path of destruction. But what?

"It would make it easier if we knew." They arrived at the tents, and Liliana crept inside.

"Well?" Sophie pounced on Celine and Liliana the moment they slipped back into the tent.

"Definitely an ogre." Liliana sat down on her bed, pulling off her boots. Putting her hand on the bed, she felt a warm, furry shape. Ardus had returned. She wondered vaguely where before collapsing into bed.

CHAPTER 20

The smell of hot buttered griddle cakes drifted into the girl's tent. Liliana cracked her eyes, rubbing away the vestiges of a sleepless night.

"Wake up, sleepyhead." Ardus crouched on her chest, a solid weight, breathing cat breath into Liliana's face.

Liliana pushed herself upright, every muscle protesting yesterday's exertions. The tent was empty. The girls must have slipped out. She dressed quickly, pulling on layers to protect against the morning chill, throwing a cloak over her shoulders. Frigid mountain air nipped her skin, raising goosebump as she shivered into Market Square. Liliana found the cook revelling in his new position as helpers buzzed around him. He had rashers of bacon, now sizzling next to neat circles of hotcakes. Soon, Liliana was sitting down with a hill of fluffy pancakes sided with bacon, ham, and strong hot milky tea and honey.

Liliana set aside a slice of bacon for Ardus, who nibbled delicately, flicking crumbs from his whiskers.

"There you are." Landry slid into the seat beside Liliana. He was fresh and clean, his hair still damp from washing.

"Hello." Liliana gulped her tea, then fanned her mouth. The tea was hot!

"Father is conducting a meeting this morning. He told me you're to join us."

"Me?" Liliana sucked in cold air, desperate to cool the burning sensation.

"Yes. Since you own the nearest estate, he feels the issue with the ogre concerns you more than anyone."

"Oh." Liliana shovelled in a forkful of griddle cake, stalling for time. Her heart flipped in her chest. What would she possibly say in a council meeting? With King Ruben. She glared at Ardus, who assumed an innocent expression.

"Of course," Ardus's smooth voice broke in before Liliana could attempt to extricate herself from the awkward situation.

Liliana frowned at the little cat, who placidly cleaned his whiskers, unconcerned with Liliana's distress.

"What time is the meeting?" Liliana pasted a bright smile on her face.

"Come as soon as you eat breakfast." Landry stole Liliana's last rasher of bacon, popping in his mouth and laughing when she gave him a dirty look.

Liliana peeked under King Ruben's tent flap, King Ruben's was the largest tent, containing not two, but three lavishly furnished rooms. Liliana's feet whispered against plush carpet as she tiptoed toward the circle seated in the king's council area.

King Ruben, Landry, Alex, Sophie, and Celine, as well as two of King Ruben's Councillors and the village headman, were seated on embroidered cushioned seats around the copper stove. Liliana blushed as all eyes fixated on her.

"Come. Sit." King Ruben smiled, gesturing toward an empty seat.

Liliana perched on the chair, adjusting the tasselled velvet cushion behind her back. Ardus followed, padding on silent feet and sitting bolt upright up on her knee.

"We're here to discuss our course of action. The ogre is a dangerous threat against the mountain villages and getting bolder every day..." King Ruben pinned the room with his gaze, all joviality dropping from his eyes. "I've sent for the sceptre; however, it won't arrive for weeks. We need to act now."

"I still think the dragons will cooperate," Celine insisted, golden hair swishing as she spoke. "You know dragons despise ogres. And I've developed a good relationship with the Iasian dragon family."

"Yes." King Ruben rubbed his chin. "But, hasn't the dragon's family egg recently hatched. You know dragons are broody with their juvenile. It's unlikely they'll leave their young, unless the ogre threatens the dragon population directly."

"What about the army?" Alex directed his question toward Captain Iain, an iron haired man with ramrod straight posture seated next to King Ruben.

"Definitely, I've sent a message to dispatch an advance guard. They will prepare a battalion if necessary. Obviously, our best course of action is to fight the ogre with as few casualties as possible. Both civilian *and* military." Captain Iain frowned.

"How long before the advance guard arrives?" Alex furrowed his brow.

"Two days for advance guard—at least. And between ten to twelve additional days for the entire battalion to arrive." Captain Iain answered.

"So effectively two weeks?" Alex said, grimacing.

"Yes." Captain Iain replied. "Obviously we'd rather come sooner, but there are logistics to put into place. The infrastructure of the mountains doesn't lend itself to sweeping in."

The group fell silent. Liliana's heat sunk, thinking of the damage and loss the ogre could inflict in a span of two weeks.

"Do you have suggestions?" King Ruben turned to Liliana.

Liliana cringed, not expecting to be put on the spot. "I suppose we should warn people," she answered slowly, hoping she wasn't covering obvious ground. "If people are expecting the ogre, they can make emergency plans. Places to hide, underground food storage, a meeting place... that sort of thing."

"A bunker." King Ruben's eyes gleamed in approval. "An excellent idea. We must create a plan and issue guards to deliver it to villages immediately." King Ruben nodded toward Iain, who tipped his head in acknowledgement.

"We also need a report on what you, Landry, and Celine saw last night. What direction was the ogre moving, his speed, things of that nature." King Ruben turned his attention to Landry.

Liliana and Landry informed King Ruben about last night's events, precious little King Ruben didn't already know. Ardus sat quietly, listening, tail twitching when Liliana mentioned the ogre seemed to search for something. They decided King Ruben's guards would warn the villages scattered through the mountain ranges.

"We'll continue our tour; people will expect us," the king decided, ignoring Iain, whose steely eyes flickered in disapproval.

"I know what you're thinking," King Ruben addressed the group. "But we can't quit just because we've come across a hiccup. People need us strong. We leave tomorrow."

Iain nodded stiffly, and the meeting adjourned. Liliana spent the rest of the day helping people sort through the wreckage. The food stores Liliana sent from the wagons would last the village for weeks; Liliana silently resolved to take advantage for more opportunities to redirect resources to the crippled village. If Ardus wanted Liliana to pretend to be the Marquis; she might as well use it to their advantage.

CHAPTER 21

The next morning, the tour left the foothills, ascending into the higher mountains. Crisp pine scented air nipped at them and the trees grew thick, shadowing the road with green light. By late afternoon, they were high, weaving through jagged rocks, moving higher—always higher. Once again, Ardus mysteriously disappeared after breakfast, leaving Liliana in the tour's company.

As she guided her horse down the narrow track, Liliana wondered how people could possibly survive the dizzying heights; there didn't seem to be farmland; it was away from well-travelled trade routes.

Liliana's question was soon answered when they met a laden wagon moving the opposite direction.

"Hello." The wagon driver tipped his cap. The wagon, hauled by two strong looking oxen, was piled with dull grey rocks, similar to the ones lining the track they had been travelling. Liliana wondered what was so special about the rocks that merited lugging them down the mountainside.

"Hello." King Ruben strode to the wagon, velvet cloak swirling, and peered over the side. "Quite the load you've got there."

"Your Majesty." The man bowed. "We've found a rich vein; I'm taking the stones to get polished and assessed by master artisans. We believe it's promising."

"Emeralds?" the king hefted a cantaloupe sized rock. Liliana noticed a flat window cut in the side of the rock. Grey with dull green streaks.

"Yes, there's beautiful stone there," the man replied.

"Whose mine's did the stones come from?" King Ruben's eyes gleamed as he spotted a deep green vein in another rock.

"The Marquis of Carabas, Your Majesty," the miner replied, twisting his dusty cap between calloused fingers.

"Ahh... of course. It would belong to the Marquis." King Ruben slid Liliana a sidelong glance before turning back to the miner. "I'm wondering, are you safe traveling alone? Why so late in the afternoon?" King Ruben asked.

The miner frowned, hesitating. "Usually we wait for an armed caravan to collect our best ore. But we've come across an.... unusual situation."

The king's head shot up. "Situation?"

"Yes." The miner scratched his cheek, eyes darting to the side. "A creature attacked us."

"... an ogre?" King Ruben finished.

"Yes. It attacked you too?"

The king nodded, eyes tightening. "It targeted the lower villages. What happened in the mining camp?"

"The ogre invaded this afternoon. Luckily, the miners were deep in the mines. Few women and children live in the mining camp; those escaped into a nearby tunnel."

"Was there extensive damage to the camp?" King Ruben asked.

"He smashed the cabins, destroyed a tunnel entrance. They aren't much anyway. We only use them in mining season. It's strange, though—he took nothing or anyone. Left as suddenly as he came. All the same, we brought the ore down the mountain in case the ogre returns. Everyone else stayed to make repairs. We can stay in one of the caves; it's been done in previous emergencies."

"Peculiar, did you have the ore in plain sight when the ogre came?"

The miner pressed his lips together. "We store ore in a safe cave that only a few know about. But there was yesterday's takings. Like I said, we've hit a rich vein. He would have noticed."

The king nodded, "We think the ogre's searching for something."

"What could he possibly be looking for? Ogre's usually want the jewels, even uncut ones."

King Ruben shook his head. "I wish we knew."

After talking a few more minutes, the miner continued down the mountain. King Ruben insisted on sending guards with him, leaving the group with only three guards and the cook. The party was subdued, each member lost in their own thoughts.

The camp was in shambles. A row of tiny wooden cabins— the miner's homes for the season— were piles of charred timber. The recent rain hadn't helped matters; everything was sodden and sticky with mud. Liliana picked her way through the muddle of scattered debris, heart sinking. How would the miners' survive this loss in the midst of their season?

Liliana spotted a tall, gangly man with red hair sorting broken crockery in the remains of a kitchen.

"Excuse me," Liliana called. She caught her sleeve on a ragged bit of wood while skirting the debris. Startled, the man leapt to his feet, then relaxed, seeing Liliana's friendly expression.

"Sorry, we're all jumpy today," he apologized, using a soggy dishcloth to wipe the grit and grime freckling his hands.

"I can see you're busy, but I was wondering if someone might show me the cave? The one you're sleeping in."

"Of course. I'll take you." The man climbed over the rubble, carrying the crockery under his arm. "Follow me."

"Wait a minute, I'll come," Landry called out. Together, they followed the man down an overgrown path. There, under a large overhanging rock, was a pocket reaching into the mountain face.

"It's bigger than you might think once you get inside." The man ducked under the rock; Liliana and Landry scrambled after him.

Once through the entrance, the cave opened to a large smooth floor, large enough to stand. It was mostly empty; every able person was repairing damage. The cave was occupied by two woman and a young boy. The women were cooking over a smouldering fire. Liliana coughed; smoke could only escape through a tiny vent in the cave roof. She stole a look around, noting piles of bedding and articles of clothing rescued from the cabin. In the back of the cave, Liliana heard rushing water and assumed there must be an underground stream deeper in the cave.

The women curtsied to Liliana and Landry; the boy bobbed in a semblance of a bow. "Thanks, Miles." One woman accepted the stack of plates of and bowls held out to her.

"Could you give them a wash?" The woman passed the crockery to the boy, who lugged them toward the underground stream.

"What are you making?" Liliana tried to make her voice friendly and gently. She glanced into the iron pot the woman was stirring and saw an unappetizing lumpy green mass.

"Lentil soup," the woman replied, continuing to stir the mixture with her wooden spoon.

"Were you able to salvage much from the wreckage?" Liliana asked. The pots didn't look full. Was this supposed to feed the entire camp?

"We recovered what we could," the woman answered. Sympathy darted through Liliana's chest. Her eyes softened. Liliana knew what it was like to have hunger gnawing at your stomach. The woman assumed a brave face but couldn't hide the worry pinching her brow.

"We can forage as well," Miles pitched in. "We're not allowed to hunt, but we can gather mushrooms and things. I have a garden as well. It's outside the camp, so it survived the attack."

Liliana pressed her lips together. Foraging was far too time consuming. They wouldn't be able to mine. And if hunting was off limits, they had few options. She saw the concern lurking in Miles' eyes.

Adelle, Miles' wife, showed Liliana and Landry around the cave. As Liliana suspected, food stores were low. If she didn't step in, they would go hungry.

"We have to help them," Liliana whispered to Landry as they picked their way down the trail toward the mining camp.

"What did you have in mind?" Landry turned his green eyes on Liliana.

"I have an idea. I need pen, oiled parchment, and a hammer and nail?"

"That's an unusual request," Landry replied, giving Liliana a curious look; however, he lost no time procuring the supplies Liliana requested. Liliana wiped off an old wooden table that somehow survived the attack and sat down to write.

Liliana folded and sealed one parchment, handing it to one of the miners to deliver to the farm. The other parchment, she nailed to a board at the camp entrance. The words were simple.

From today, miners and servants of Marquis of Carabas may hunt these mountain lands. Signed—Marquis of Carabas

Landry read the sign out loud, shooting Liliana a look of approval.

"The food won't arrive for a few days," Liliana explained. "Hopefully this will help the miners survive."

Liliana smiled, pushing away uneasy thoughts. What would the real Marquis think when he heard she allowed hunting on his lands? If this is what kept people sheltered and fed, it would be worth it.

CHAPTER 22

"I wish we had more to offer."

Liliana lugged a sack of beans down the rutted path leading toward the miner's cave. The sun hung low in the sky. Liliana and the tour had spent the entire afternoon helping the miners recover from the ogre's damage. They stored all salvageable food in the cave, safe and dry. Several of the miners set out on a hunting expedition. The forest mountainsides were full of game; the hunters returned with venison and game hens. They added meat to the lentil stew, drying the rest in strips stretched on woven mats. They would store the dried meat with the other food.

"What you've done is a lifeline." Landry ducked through the gloomy cave entrance, hefting a burlap sack from his muscled shoulder. Even the royal family joined the effort to repair the mining camp; King Ruben accompanied the hunt, bringing down a large buck. Landry muttered to Liliana that King Ruben would brag about his accomplishment for months; it almost wasn't worth the meat to be forced to listen to his crowing.

"I wish I could fix it all." Liliana stared at the ruins of the cabins with sorrowful eyes.

"There is something you could do," Landry spoke slowly.

"What?"

"Nothing substantial, but I overheard the miners discussing how they would have lumber sent from the plains because there's a ban on cutting trees here."

"There is? I mean, oh that." Liliana caught her near slip. She tilted her head. "I can lift the ban." Liliana lost no time in calling for parchment, pen, and ink. She wrote a new notice, signing with a flourish and nailing it at the village entrance.

"There." Liliana stepped back with satisfaction to l examine her work. This will help them get back on their feet. Any trouble stemming from the notices would rest on her head. Liliana shivered, pushing apprehensive thoughts away, not wanting to consider what might happen when her lies came crashing down around her. At least she would have done something useful. Something worthwhile.

Ardus wound his way around Liliana's feet, rubbing her ankles until she gave in and picked him up, tucking the cat inside her cloak.

"We're travelling into in Antarai territory tomorrow," Landry remarked, leaning against a crooked fencepost.

"Have you visited the Antarai before?" Liliana asked.

Landry shook his head. "We didn't venture that far last tour. The Antarai keep to themselves; they don't involve themselves with outsiders too much. But they've been at the castle recently and seem friendly. Brought lovely gifts." Landry threw Liliana a pointed look.

"Father really wanted Celine to understand all of Iasia. And he wants to see if the Antarai sustained damage from the ogre."

Liliana stroked the soft spot under Ardus's chin, wondering how her Antarai friends had fared against the ogre.

"How extensive is Antarai territory?"

"It covers from these ranges to the Western border. To be honest, we'd like to learn more about the Antarai. They were interested in trade at one point, but Penelope offended them, and they dropped the agreement," Landry said, frowning.

"Did you ever find out what happened between them and Penelope?"

Landry shook his head, "No, but it was dreadful. I know people think the Antarai are warlike, but they didn't fight; they just left and refused contact until..."

"Until what?" Liliana asked.

"Until you and that cat of yours came along. They must have warmed up to you. Was your estate near a settlement?"

Liliana tensed, holding Ardus's warm body to her chest. She desperately wished she could end the charade and tell Landry the entire story. But that would ruin everything. She glanced at Ardus, who narrowed his eyes, giving her a warning look.

"I suppose I've seen Antarai near the estate sometimes," Liliana almost choked as she pushed the words out of her mouth.

A look of understanding crossed Landry's face. "That's how you knew them. What were the Antarai like?"

"Different," Liliana answered. "Different, but lovely. Loyal, welcoming, and their hunting and bushcraft skills are amazing."

"And magic?" An intent expression flashed across Landry's face.

"Yes. Magic, too. Although I don't know a lot about their magic, except that they practice. They have a seer for sure, but other mages as well." Although the Antarai were secretive about what magic they had access to, Liliana suspected it was significantly more than shown to her.

The two wandered back to the campsite, drawn toward the smell of roasted venison floating through the cool evening air. Milot outdid himself, covering the venison with fresh herbs and roasting it over a spit before putting it between two rounds of flatbread baked over coals. Liliana took her portion underneath a large awning set up as a resting area for those repairing the camp. She moved a bucket of tools to make a space on the wooden bench beside Celine.

"I hear you've been the busy bee today." Celine bit into her flatbread, washing it down with a gulp of spiced tea.

"I couldn't sit by and do nothing." Liliana inhaled her flatbread, the warm fluffy bread a delicious counterpart to the herbs and venison.

"You wouldn't catch Sophie getting her hands dirty for her estate." Celine threw her brother-in-law a cheeky grin. The tips of Landry's ears glowed red as he concentrated on his plate.

"Where is Sophie?" Liliana noticed the other girl was missing.

"Sophie complained about a headache," Landry answered, stiffening with disapproval. "She's lying down in her tent."

Alex smirked at his brother's discomfort. "You remember how Sophie followed you around all last year like a lost puppy—you didn't complain about Sophie then."

"I couldn't be rude." Landry protested. "Her father is an Earl. An important Earl. And on the trade committee. Mother would be furious if I offended him."

Liliana's heart sank as she watched the lighthearted banter between brothers; she hadn't considered Landry and Sophie might have a prior relationship, but of course, why *wouldn't* they? Landry was attractive, single, and a *prince*. And Sophie was beautiful, cultured, rich, and knowledgeable about the court. Everything Liliana wasn't. The bread and meat stuck in her throat, dry and flavourless in her mouth.

Liliana glanced up; Landry's green eyes were fixed on her, an apologetic expression hiding in their depths. She turned her face, avoiding the pity she imagined. How silly to assume there could be something between them. It's not like Liliana was actually the Marquis of Carabas. Just an imposter, when they discovered she was the daughter of a mere village tradesman, everything would be over. The realization sliced her like a knife.

Liliana choked down the rest of her meal in silence, fighting the tears threatening to clog her throat.

"I'm exhausted." Liliana stretched her arms overhead, putting a hand over her mouth in pretence of a yawn. "If we're leaving early, I should get some sleep." She stood and left the shelter, relieved for the darkness hiding her tears.

"Liliana, wait." Landry jogged behind her. "Liliana, what Celine said about Sophie. It doesn't mean what you think."

Liliana choked out a laugh."I don't know what you're talking about." It took all her effort to make her voice sound airy and light.

"Sophie and I. At one time, I thought there was something between us. But it meant nothing. Not really," Landry insisted.

"Landry." Liliana turned, eyes glittering in the pale moonlight. "If you and Sophie have something between you, that's fine with me. You're free to do whatever you want to do." The words sliced her throat like daggers as she forced them past her lips. After all, Liliana wouldn't be a fake Marquis forever; it would break her heart to leave him behind. Landry could return to court, find a nice girl from the nobility. He'd forget the funny country girl with the false title. She'd be a dinner party tale. A story to entertain guests.

Liliana spun and ran down the path, hot tears running silently down her cheeks. Landry remained frozen where she left him, watching in silence as Liliana disappeared into her tent. Throwing herself on her cot, she gave into the sadness. Eventually, she felt a warm presence as a solid weight settled by her side.

"Don't worry." Ardus spoke in a soothing voice. "Everything will work out, you'll see." He moved closer, letting Liliana comfort herself by clutching him to her side. Eventually, tears still on her cheeks, she fell into a fitful sleep.

CHAPTER 23

The morning sun blazed high, and they were folding the tents, rolling them into the tent cases.

"You know how King Ruben is." Celine giggled, rolling her eyes. King Ruben gave them a suspicious look from his table across the campground.

"It's like he knows we're talking about him," Liliana said. She'd woken up this morning determined to enjoy the rest of this adventure, pushing all thoughts of Landry out of her head. She should have known better anyway. Liliana felt a prickle on her neck and glanced up to see his thoughtful green eyes regarding her solemnly. Liliana jerked the cords that fastened her bedroll and turned her face away.

"I wouldn't like to trade places with that bedroll." Celine glanced at the offending item. "What's wrong? You left so quickly last night."

"Nothing," Liliana insisted, stuffing items of clothing into a saddlebag. "I'm just excited to get moving. That's all."

Celine said nothing, merely sliding her a skeptical glance. "It looks as though it may be awhile before we leave. Do you want a practice with me?"

"Practice?" Liliana questioned, eying the sword hanging at Celine's side. "Do you mean with the sword?"

"Yes. I can get you an extra sword from the guards."

"Are you sure? I've never used a sword before." Liliana threw the sword a suspicious look.

"No time like the present. I find it's the best way to get rid of any extra.... energy." Celine grinned, adding the last comment with a diplomatic tone.

"All right. I'll try." Liliana took the hand Celine offered, letting the princess pull her up. Minutes later, she found herself standing in the clearing next to the old ore shed facing Celine, who had a determined glint flashing in her eyes.

"Hold the sword like this." Celine arranged Liliana's hands around the handle of the weapon. Liliana faltered, the heavy sword felt awkward and unfamiliar in her hand. "Then, put your feet here, and move from the hips. It means you react faster when you need to be quick."

After showing Liliana the basic moves, Celine stood back, encouraging her to try.

Liliana jabbed the air, her movements slow and unfamiliar.

"Well done." Celine clapped. "You're a natural. You'll pick it up in no time."

Liliana glowed under the praise of the golden princess. She had to admit, it felt good to swing the weapon; although, it would take practice, a lot of practice, before she would be even close to proficient.

"I see Celine's converting you to Lovanian swordplay." Alex and Landry strode across the clearing. Celine leaned up for a kiss from her husband, and Landry and Liliana exchanged uncomfortable glances.

"I'm definitely a beginner, but hopefully I'll start picking up some skills soon." Liliana grinned.

"We'll practice again tomorrow. I think they sent these two to hint that it's time to leave."

Soon, the touring party set off. Because the road would all but disappear by the time they reached their eventual destination, they left the carriages and bulkier items in the mining camp, travelling solely by horseback.

They climbed steadily, the thin sharp air burned Liliana's lungs, but it was spiced with pine and the undefinable scent of wild mountain air. The path twisted through valleys and peaks, making it hard to see far in the distance. The group was on edge, the recent ogre attacks raised tensions.

"Wait." Rustling in the trees caught Liliana's ear.

Everyone stopped. The only sound was wind rushing through branches, mingling with the breathing and stomping of horses.

Crash.

Shattering branches and crackling underbrush sounded nearby. Something plunged through the forest. Something big. One of the horses whinnied, startled by the noise. There was nowhere to run; the path was too steep and narrow. Liliana felt every muscle tense as the guards drew their swords, preparing to fight.

The group poised collectively as the creature approached. Out of the underbrush leapt a Jokai, a huge elk with wide spreading antlers, towering over even the tallest of their horses. The creature raised its elegant head, sniffing the wind, its breathy tendrils of steam suspended in air.

Liliana had never seen a creature that large or that magnificent in her life. She drew in a sharp breath, spellbound by its beauty and grandeur. One of the guards raised his sword.

"No!" Liliana shouted, a fierce sense of protectiveness rising in her chest. "Leave the creature alone."

Startled by her cry, the creature tossed its antlers and sprang away, floating over the underbrush in one leap.

"It's not hurting anyone," she explained, squirming under the weight of everyone's eyes bearing on her. "And it's so beautiful." The guard slid his sword back into its scabbard.

King Ruben nodded. "Just right, dear. We wouldn't be able to carry it with us, anyway." He motioned for the group to continue their journey.

Mood subdued, the group climbed, spiraling higher and higher in the peaks. It was late when they finally arrived at the first Antarai village, a cluster of three large huts fashioned of split wood and woven reeds. They were roofed with long dried grasses tied together. Each hut could house twenty to thirty people.

Liliana watched thin filaments of smoke rising from different sections of the huts. She assumed each family must have their own kitchen area. Nearby enclosures held animals, shaggy ponies the Antarai were so fond of, and cattle, hardy animals with shaggy russet coats and widespread horns needling into wicked points.

A chorus of barking alerted the Antarai to the party's arrival. Shortly, a group of Antarai came and greeted them, dressed in their most colourful embroidery.

Sokdi arrived first, long black hair streaming in the wind like ribbons of silk. She stood straight and proud, the gleam in her eyes and the curve of her lips giving away how glad she was to see Liliana again.

Yingyai had no such reservations. "Lili," he greeted her effusively, squeezing her so tight she gasped for breath. "I'm so happy you're finally here."

Liliana stepped back, eyes narrowed, "You knew I was coming?"

"Of course." Yingyai grinned, eyes dancing. "Come. I'll show you around the huts."

Leaving their horses in the care of Tommy, a young groom Princess Celine had taken under her wing, and two young Antarai boys, Liliana and the group followed the Antarai welcome party down a stony path leading toward the huts. Up close, the huts looked like huge grass domes. Yingyai ducked through a tiny doorway, so low even Liliana had to crouch to get inside.

Once in, Liliana gaped in amazement. The hut was even bigger inside that she originally assumed. The dome stretched two stories up with a covered courtyard in the center. And it was crowded. Every inch of the space taken with bedding, cooking areas, each family with their own square firepit, and children. So many children.

A tiny girl around three years old peeked from behind her mother's brightly patterned skirt, dark eyes full of curiosity. Liliana knelt, holding out her hand to the little girl.

"Hello," Liliana softened her voice. "What's your name?"

The little girl shrank, face uncertain, until her mother spoke to her rapidly in the liquid Antarai tongue.

"Sheesha," the girl's voice was high and sweet as her face broke into a gap-toothed smile. She tucked a dimpled thumb in her mouth as she clung to her mother's leg.

Liliana wished she'd brought a treat or toy, something to share with Sheesha. She felt in her pockets, disappointed to find only lint gathered on the bottom seam.

"Soi," the little girl spoke the word in a high, clear voice. She reached out a chubby hand to stroke Ardus's soft fur. Ardus sat patiently, letting the child run sticky fingers down his back.

Liliana smiled at the little girl who, curiosity satisfied, dashed away to join the children playing in the courtyard.

"We usually only have twenty people living in a baan this size," Sokdi explained as Liliana stood. "But the ogre outright destroyed several villages, so everyone lives here temporarily. Not that we mind." She smiled apologetically at Sheesha's mother, who merely shrugged.

"How many villages did the ogre destroy?" Liliana examined the hut interior, that explained why it was crammed with people and belongings.

"Four villages on this mountain peak were completely flattened, and three villages need repairs, but those can crowd together until they've completed rebuilding."

"Have you noticed a path that the ogre takes? Why did he destroy the other villages but skip this one?" King Ruben shed his usual jovial attitude as he absorbed the information. He focused on Sokdi, giving her his complete attention.

"We have noticed the attacks centre around a certain area. As for the ogre skipping this village, it's because we have a mage who casts an invisibility cloak."

"Really?" King Ruben's eyes sharpened. A mage this powerful and advanced was rare in the Iasian lowlands.

Sokdi nodded. "He can't keep the invisibility cloak up long though; the effort would exhaust him, but he can sustain the cloak until the ogre passes. The ogre's been back twice since, so clearly it suspects our village is in this location. We've had to be extra vigilant. Right now, we've a rotation of night guards. And obviously the mage can't leave the settlement. He has to stay here to protect the village."

King Ruben appeared impressed at the Antarai's strategy and skill. "I would like to meet this mage. Is that a possibility?"

"Of course." Sokdi glided away, whispering instructions to a group of men hovering nearby. They cast sidelong glances at the new arrivals before they scurried to follow her bidding.

"Is it true? About the mage?" King Ruben whispered to Liliana.

"If Sokdi says so, it must be true," Liliana answered. Although she hadn't known about the mage with the invisibility cloak, Sokdi had never, to Liliana's knowledge, embellished the truth. In fact, quite the opposite. Sokdi downplayed the unusual abilities of the Antarai.

Sokdi reappeared, following in her wake a young man, only in his early twenties. Long shiny black hair fell in waves to the tops of his shoulders; he was blinking sleepily, a pillow crease lining one cheek.

"This is Maihen." The man bowed gracefully, unsurprised by the unusual guests.

"I hear you cast an invisibility cloak," King Ruben addressed Maihen.

"Yes," Maihen answered. His dark eyes were steady as they met King Ruben's gaze.

"Fascinating." King Ruben gazed at Mailin with admiration. "I would love to see it sometime. It's a skill I've heard of, but I've never seen it practiced. Such a wonderful thing you're doing for your people."

"Thank you." Mailin looked bewildered by the king's effusive compliments.

Liliana took the chance to slide between Sokdi and Yingyai. "How are you?" she squeezed Sokdi's arm. "Can we talk?" She slid her eyes around the rest of the group, still distracted by Maihen and his unusual talents.

Sokdi nodded, leading Liliana to a quiet corner near a firepit. A few children played nearby, and Sokdi sent them away, grumbling with a flick of her hand.

"What is it, my friend?" Sokdi's large dark eyes searched Liliana's face.

Liliana let out a deep breath, relieved someone finally knew who she really was. Just Liliana, the miller's sister. Not a marquis. Not a hero. Not a rescuer. She hadn't realized how heavy the burden was until she saw the Antarai and remembered the freedom she had with them.

"It's just," Liliana paused, tracing a pattern on the hewn wooded floor with her toe. "They all think I'm the Marquis, and it's terrifying me. I feel awful deceiving them."

"Ah, you care for them? These royals." Sokdi tipped her head.

"Yes." Liliana hadn't realized the truth until the word slipped out of her mouth.

"What does your cat Ardus say?"

"He says to wait. Just for a little while longer." Liliana's shoulder's slumped.

"I see," Sokdi paused, a thoughtful expression flickering in her eyes. "And do you feel you can wait a little longer?"

"If I have to. But I'm scared about how angry they're going to be when they learn the truth." Liliana furrowed her brow.

"Of course, that's understandable. You wouldn't feel that if you didn't truly care for them." Sokdi laid a gentle hand on Liliana's arm. "You must do what you feel is best. But, if you wait, if you trust Ardus, they will see your heart and forgive you. King Ruben is a good man."

Liliana chewed her lip, staring at the glowing coals clustered in the firepit. "I'll have to think about it."

Sokdi nodded. "Whatever you decide, we Antarai believe in you." She stood, brushing a streak of soot from her long colourful skirt and moved away.

Although the Antarai invited the party to stay with them in the largest hut, the touring party opted to set up tents in a nearby clearing. Instead, they joined the Antarai for dinner, sitting cross-legged on woven mats spread across the floor. Liliana relished the return to Antarai food. She had missed the spiced smoky flavours and the wild forest ingredients. King Ruben's cook was especially fascinated. After marvelling at the flavours and textures, he insisted on being led to the kitchen—amazed when he saw a firepit with a simple iron trivet. He came away with a linen sack stuffed full of ingredients, spices, and the brown lentil bean that was a staple in the Antarai diet.

Satisfied by the food and the company, Liliana relaxed, leaning against the smoothly woven reeds of the inner wall. Ardus lay content in her lap, purring as she stroked his soft fur. It was then she heard it. A faint rumble vibrating the hut.

"What was that?" Celine, sitting next to her, sat up abruptly. She wasn't the only one to notice the disturbance. A hush fell over the room as everyone strained to listen. Again, the rumble, this time Liliana felt the wall tremble; something very large and very heavy was shaking the earth.

"Is that?" Liliana looked at Celine, whose eyes were wide. Her hand hovered above her sword, poised to strike if needed.

"I think so," Celine whispered, tension radiating from her slight form.

"Bring Maihen," Lukdee whispered, his voice thick with tension.

But Maihen was already there. Liliana watched, mingled interest and fear racing through her veins as Maihen sat in the middle of the room. The older Antarai, both men and women, circled him, joining hands. In complete silence, they closed their eyes as Maihen's face creased in concentration.

A flicker of energy slithered through the hut, that familiar twinge as the air swirled with magic. Liliana glanced down. Her hands looked different, like a shimmering veil had crossed in front of her face. The air felt liquid, everything slowed, suspended.

A bead of sweat rolled down the side of Maihen's temple as the creature rumbled closer. Closer. Liliana hardly dared breathe, in case the ogre heard. The smell of rotten meat, the stench Liliana smelled when she and Landry saw the ogre in the forest, filled the air—pungent, caustic seeping through the walls. A child whimpered and was quickly shushed by its mother.

Then she heard the raspy breath. In and out. In and out. The ogre sniffed the air. A growl split the air.

"I know you're here." The stench grew stronger, nearly unbearable, cloying, so thick Liliana could almost see it rolling in waves through the air.

Ardus tensed, every hair on his back raised, his compact form going rigid in her arms, Liliana ran a soothing hand down his back, comforting him.

Still closer, goosebumps ran up Liliana's arms as the creature shuffled, harsh breathing the only sound breaking the silence.

"I'll find you yet, you mangy fleabag," the creature roared. The walls trembled under the force. Liliana squeezed her eyes shut.

The creature roared again, something crashed. It tore a tree from the earth and threw it, shattering the night with destruction. Then the creature took out its rage on the forest, staying away from their protective bubble. Liliana saw the effort was taking its toll on Maihen, whose olive coloured skin took on a waxy sheen, his eyes squeezed tight with the effort of keeping his people shielded.

Finally, the ogre lumbered away, muttering threats under its breath. Liliana's heartbeat slowed, and she felt Ardus relax under her hand.

Maihen cracked opened his eyes, exhausted and pale. The Antarai elders were also suffering from the effort of sustaining Maihen's effort. They gathered around him, murmuring, one supporting him as he sank to the floor. Two elders propped Maihen between them, guiding him to a bed in a quiet corner, gently covering him with a gaily patterned blanket. Maihen's eyes drifted shut the moment his head hit the pillow.

"How long can Maihen shield the settlement?" Liliana whispered to Sokdi, who'd slipped between her and Celine.

"I'm not sure." Sokdi's face was drawn and pinched. "This is the longest he's ever shielded, and I think it's pushed him to his limit."

CHAPTER 24

"How does the invisibility cloak work?" Celine asked, wide blue eyes full of questions.

"The invisibility cloak is like a net; Maihen throws it over the area with his mind. It repels anyone and anything from outside his net; that's how the trees missed us. The cloak masks sound, but we stay quiet, so Maihen can concentrate. Any distraction can make his concentration slip," Sokdi explained.

The Antarai men moved toward the tiny doorway, heading outside the hut to assess damages. King Ruben and Alex accompanied them. Liliana peeked out the narrow doorway. The ogre had ravaged the area surrounding the village. Trees were ripped out by the roots and scattered across the forest. Some of them splintered, Liliana realised with a lurch. They had been used as clubs. But it was like Sokdi explained; the animals and the huts were completely spared.

"Has the ogre been here many times?" Celine turned back to Sokdi.

"This is the fourth. We think he's holing up nearby."

"And what is the ogre searching for?" Celine asked.

Sokdi merely shook her head, a helpless expression in her eyes.

They slept fitfully. Even in her sleep, the ogre never left Liliana, haunting her with fiery breath and grasping hands, squeezing, shattering, breaking.... She woke with a start. Sweat pooled underneath her.

Breathing heavily, Liliana took in her surroundings. Everything was dark, the only sound was the soft breathing of the girls sleeping in the tent. Next to her, she felt the warm solid body of the little cat; he tapped her with his paw.

"I know what the ogre's searching for," Ardus voice was small. Unsure.

"You do? What?"

"Me."

"You?" Liliana's mouth gaped.

"Yes," the little cat whispered.

"But.... *why*?" Liliana stroked the little cat, feeling the fine bones underneath the flesh and fur.

"I have something she wants."

Liliana wondered what the ogre wanted from her mysterious little cat.

"What will you do about it?" Liliana lowered her voice as Sarah mumbled and shifted in the next cot.

"Defeat her," the little cat answered. "It's the only way."

Liliana gulped. How they would defeat a creature so large, so vicious... so strong... was beyond her wildest imagination.

"*Now*?"

Ardus yawned as he settled back down beside her. "No, we leave in the morning." At that, the cat sleepily closed his eyes and fell asleep.

"Ardus, what is going on? I've done everything you asked and I think by now you owe me an explanation." Liliana answered, huffing.

Ardus placed a furry paw on Liliana's arm. "I wish I could, I really do, but I promised my Master to keep his secrets. I made an *oath*. A cat keeps his oath." He said, his green eyes glowing.

"But...." Liliana said, feeling the frustration rise.

"Liliana, have I led you wrong? Hasn't everything worked out, I brought you this far, trust me. I'll explain everything the minute I'm released from my oath, I promise."

"Fine, but I want to know everything, and I mean every, single detail." Liliana said in a firm voice.

"That sounds fair." Ardus curled up and fell asleep beside her.

Liliana lay awake, eyes wide open. It wasn't until near dawn she finally fell into a fitful sleep.

The Antarai invited the party to breakfast with them in the main hut—spicy bean cakes, and the usual porridge with toppings. Liliana dived into her breakfast, enjoying the taste and texture; although, she noticed after a few bites, King Ruben set his spoon back in the bowl, insisting he was full.

After breakfast, the elders gathered in the smallest hut, sitting cross-legged in a circle on woven mats. They invited King Ruben and Alex along with Celine to join. Landry cast a longing glance at the gathering, yearning to join the discussion, but they invited only the most senior royals.

Sokdi was leading gathering of the elders and Liliana found herself at loose ends. Liliana settled for helping the younger Antarai at the firepits, determined to learn the spices that made Antarai food so delicious. Landry had wandered in, avoiding Sophie's sighing gazes and decided to help.

"Is it strange your brother is in the meeting and you're here?" Liliana asked Landry.

"I suppose. I'm used to it now." Landry wiped a copper pot, hanging it on a hook.

Liliana nodded, pinching off a piece of a small pointy red vegetable and putting it in her mouth. Fire immediately exploded on her tongue, making her choke and cough.

"Are you all right?" Landry took in the watering eyes and red cheeks.

"Water," gasped Liliana. She grabbed a cup and dipped it in the water jug, drinking deeply. "What was that?" she examined the offending vegetable.

"It looks like a chilli. They're what makes the food have heat. We had some at the estate. Used them for practical jokes."

"That was definitely heat." Liliana shuddered. She wouldn't be putting one of those in her mouth again.

"Excuse me, Lady Liliana." Liliana turned to a young Antarai woman beckoning gracefully. "You're needed in the gathering."

A dart of anxiety shot through Liliana as she wondered what the elders could want her for. Deciding she needed support, she scooped up Ardus, peacefully sunning himself, and headed toward the meeting.

"Welcome." Sokdi gestured for her to wedge in beside her.

Liliana bowed her head, sitting cross-legged.

"We ask you to grant us a favour," Tailuk spoke.

"Of course," Liliana wondered what she was agreeing to.

"We believe the ogre is headed for the Carabas estate," Sokdi continued.

Liliana waited, a lump growing heavy in her chest.

"We ask you to take us to the estate. We know its location is off limits; only the household of the Marquis of Carabas is privy to it, but we ask that you make allowances. When the ogre is defeated, we will leave you and your family in peace." Sokdi's eyes pleaded with Liliana to go along with the ruse.

"Of course," Liliana agreed, ignoring the lurch in her stomach.

A collective sigh of relief filtered around the room. Liliana wondered how she would ever find the secret estate. How would the true Marquis react when Liliana arrived at the Carabas Estate as an imposter?

"I will accompany my Mistress when we lead you to the Carabas Estate." Ardus sat up regally, holding his head erect. "But we need three days to travel ahead and prepare."

"What, a helpless woman alone, with the ogre rampaging. I refuse to entertain the idea," King Ruben spoke.

"I guarantee we will stay well out the creature's path. But, if you insist, we will bring one, and only one, person with us." Ardus stared at the king, green eyes filled with determination.

"Three days," King Ruben's tone was final.

"That will do." The cat settled on Liliana's knee.

CHAPTER 25

"I certainly hope you know what you're doing," Liliana grumbled as she packed her bag.

"Of course, I do." Ardus sat on the bedroll, cleaning his whiskers.

"And you promise me, when we get to the estate and do whatever it is we have to do, this will all be over?" Liliana gave him a hard look.

"Certainly," Ardus agreed smoothly.

Before she had time to think, Liliana was climbing up on her horse. She bit her lip, stomach churning. She had no idea which way she was going, or what she was going to do when she got there.

"Trust me," Ardus purred, settling himself in front of her.

"*You're* the one coming with me?" Liliana turned in her saddle toward Landry, who grinned unrepentantly.

"You don't have to look so excited about it," he complained good naturedly, adjusting his stirrups.

"I'm just surprised... that's all." Liliana felt a blush creeping up her neck. She hadn't meant to make him feel unwelcome. The butterflies exploded at the thought of having to face the rightful marquis in front of Landry.

"Trust me," Ardus whispered, sensing her distress.

With a cheeky wink, Landry followed her out of the camp. From horseback, the devastation of the forest around the camp could be seen even more clearly. Liliana felt her heart break as she saw the devastation of the carefully tended Antarai gardens; everything was smashed to bits.

"Is this going to stop the ogre?" she asked Ardus.

"If we play our cards right, it will. I have a plan, and I think it's a good one, but I might need your help." Liliana felt the tension radiating from the little cat.

"Of course." Liliana gave the small animal a comforting pat.

With Ardus's directions, they were soon winding their way up a steep mountain path. The air was chilly so high up, and their breath sent white tendrils floating up into the sky. They stopped briefly for a meal of dried meat and flatbread, letting the horses rest before moving on. If they weren't on such a serious mission and if she didn't have such a huge lie hanging over her head, Liliana would have enjoyed the journey. The sky was so blue, the forest was beautiful in all its wildness, and the company was pleasant. Liliana wished with all her heart that she didn't have that lie standing between her and Landry, but what if she didn't. He wasn't likely to look at her, a mere commoner.

"What's wrong? You look like you have the weight of the world on your shoulders." Landry coaxed her, distracting her from her reverie.

"I suppose I do have a lot on my mind." Liliana toyed with the idea of letting the truth all spill out, the thought filling her with the mixed anticipation of terror and relief. But where would that leave her. Her loyalty was to Ardus. She pressed her lips firmly together. "Do you ever wish things were different?" her eyes, liquid with emotion, searched Landry's green ones.

Landry cocked his head, thinking. "I have. But I'm not sure what you are talking about."

"I'm just...not the person you think I am." She skated around the truth.

Landry chuckled. "I don't think any of us are."

Liliana felt the little cat tense against her. "Later, now is not the time," Ardus whispered under his breath. Liliana said nothing, concentrating on the neck of the horse in front of her.

"I suppose," she said after a long pause.

After some time, the terrain began to change. It was still thick pine, but the path was less steep and wider, pebbles replacing the sharp boulder like rocks. There were even patches of green grass between the trees, interspersed with meadows. Eventually, the track broadened until it could nearly be called a road. In front of her, Ardus perked up, his bright golden eyes sharp and watchful.

Then, they saw it. Around a bend loomed a large castle, multiple spires rising into the sky.

"Is this the manor?" Landry whistled under his breath. "I was expecting something a bit more modest."

Anxiety twisted in Liliana's stomach as they approached the enormous building, its shadow raising the hairs on the back of her neck and sending goosebumps chasing across her skin.

There was no one there.

The place was completely empty. Liliana led her horse across the lowered drawbridge, expecting at any minute to be stopped by a guard, but the only sounds were the hoofbeats that echoed hollow across the wooden bridge.

"Is it always like this?" Landry looked around, concern flitting across his face.

"I don't think so...." Liliana answered. At the other end of the drawbridge stood an empty guardhouse, the door swinging open in the breeze. Liliana peeked inside, but it too was empty, the only sign that it had once been occupied was a sheaf of parchment, now yellow and stained by time. It was clear by the thick layer of dust that this place had been abandoned for some time.

"When's the last time you've been here?" Landry gave her a suspicious look.

"Umm.." Liliana's voice faltered. She was so tired of lying, she didn't even begin to know how to answer this question. "Not for a while." The end of her sentence came out like a question.

"I can see that." Landry pointedly eyed the dusty windows and rusty metal. "Do you want to go inside. Maybe see where everyone is?" He started across the ghostly courtyard toward the front door that yawned open in front of them. It was too dark to see in until they got to the door. The inside of the courtyard was as empty as the outside. Again, thick dust covered every surface. One of the marble statues lay broken, jagged pieces scattering the floor with white shards.

"I wonder what happened?" Landry squinted through the gloom.

Liliana wondered too, but didn't dare speak the words out loud.

Landry continued on, leaving a trail of footprints across the black and white marble. The entry led to a great hall, nearly the size of King Ruben and Queen Abigail's throne room. It was entirely polished white marble, now grey with disuse. A row of windows revealed the landscape of towering mountains, their height dwarfing the castle as they rose into the sky.

A dais presided at the front of the room. White marble steps lead to the ornate thronelike chair, also in white. But that is not what drew their attention. What drew their attention was the mirror. A giant, polished mirror, bounced light from the windows off its gleaming surface, flinging splinters of light around the room. Liliana drew close to the mirror, reaching a tentative hand to touch the ornate frame.

"Stop." Landry grabbed her arm before she could make contact.

Stunned, Liliana jerked her hand away.

"Sorry." Landry frowned. "It's just, I think that's a magic mirror. And if it is, it's very powerful."

Liliana looked at the mirror with awe. She had heard of the magic mirror, each of the magical kingdoms used to have one. Never had she imagined she would see one in real life.

"How do you know?" Liliana asked.

"I can feel it. It's like a tingle; it almost stings."

Liliana narrowed her eyes, concentrating on the shimmering surface of the mirror. The surface began to cloud, a fog rippling across the smooth surface." Then, she felt it. A buzzing sensation, not completely unpleasant, that moved across her skin. She let out a sharp breath and moved closer.

"Don't look at it too close either," Landry warned.

Liliana jerked her head away, squeezing her eyes shut tight.

"Will we keep going?" Landry motioned toward a door at the far end of the room. Silently, Liliana followed him across the room, accompanied by Ardus, whose little cat feet left a trail of tiny prints across the floor.

The entire grounds were the same. Once fine rooms, beginning to decay. Even the stables were empty; the bins were full of mouldering grain, and the hay had turned black with age and damp.

"Not even a mouse. I don't understand it. Where did everybody go?" Landry wondered as they looked through the kitchen. A bag of potatoes had rotted on the large kitchen table, and a peeler lay abandoned as if someone had been interrupted in their task.

After exploring stables and the main floor, they moved to the outbuildings. It was here that they found what they didn't know they had been looking for. Behind the stable was a large carriage house. A prickle of warning crept up Liliana's spine when she spotted the heavy wooden doors—doors large enough to bring a carriage through—hanging off their hinges. It was as if they had been torn off, by something very large and very, very strong.

They noticed the smell first. Pungent, overpowering, rotten. Liliana's first instinct was to turn and dash for the door, back out into the clean, crisp, sunlight. But she forced herself to move forward, one step at a time, into the murky depths of the carriage house. The carriages were gone, although some remnants remained, a wheel here, a few bits of tack hanging on the walls there. Whatever was there had clearly been torn apart to make room for... what *was* that? Liliana crept closer, a pile of rags had been pushed into a sort of bed. If you could even call it a bed.

"Do you think this is it?" Liliana whispered to Landry. Even at a whisper, her voice felt too loud.

"It certainly seems so. Look at this." Landry motioned for Liliana to come closer.

"What *is* that?" Liliana recoiled at a pile of feathers stuck to the remains of a kind of animal lying on the floor.

"It's hard to tell now, but those look like swan feathers."

Liliana took a hasty step back and put a hand over her nose, trying to block out the stench. They were so distracted, they didn't even notice the shadow crossing the large open doorway. A slam, as a large hand flung the door right off its hinges. It skidded across the floor, only screeching to a halt when it slammed against the back wall and groaned to a halt.

"I know you're in here." The ogre stood in the doorway, its shadow blocking all of the available light with its bulk. Its nose twitched, sniffing the air. Weaving its head back and forth, it searched the room with its beady eyes.

Liliana froze, standing in the centre of the room like a target; but Landry pulled her back. They crouched behind a dividing wall. He caught her eye, then flicked his head to the right. Slowly, slowly, one excruciating inch at a time, she turned her head. Behind her was a rickety staircase. The carriage master's quarters.

Landry put his mouth next to her ear. "I'll distract it, then we'll make a break for it."

The ogre ducked its head, crouching to get into the space. "Where are you, you mangy animal? I know you're in here, and we're going to have it out once and for all."

Landry and Liliana exchanged a look. Where was Ardus? Her eyes frantically searched the room, looking for any sign of the little cat, but he had disappeared, melting into the darkness like a wraith.

The ogre roared and stomped his great tree sized leg, causing the rafters to creak. "You're so close, and you won't get away from me this time." The creature growled before turning to the pile of rags that made his bed, tearing into them.

"Now. And Quietly," whispered Landry. Holding her hand tight he ran for the stairs, feet soundless on the straw littered floor. They were so close, three steps from the top, before they were seen or heard. It was the squeaky stair that gave them away. The ogre spun around, ears twitching. He lunged up the stair after them. Liliana scrambled behind Landry through the first room they saw and slammed the door shut behind them. Crash, the ogre slammed against the door and it began to splinter. The room was small— a small bed, a few pegs on the wall and a chest of drawers were the only thing in it. One small window, too small to squeeze through, faced them.

Landry dived under the bed, pulling Liliana behind him, and they crouched there. Pressed up against the wall, Liliana's heart beat frantically, so loud she was sure the ogre must be able to hear it.

The door shattered, ripped from it hinges, and flew across the room with a bang. The rotten putrid smell filled the air. Liliana desperately wanted to gag from the odor but didn't dare.

An evil chuckle rippled through the air and the bed was flung across the room in one fell swoop, leaving Landry and Liliana exposed. Hot breath fanned her cheek, as the ogre leaned over to look at her. She cowered against the wall, wondering if these were to be her last moments.

"Where is he?" the ogre growled.

"Who?" Liliana asked, refusing to betray her little friend.

"Don't toy with me, little girl. I can smell him." The ogre roared as he smashed the chest of drawers with his fist.

"Looking for someone?" Ardus picked his way over the fragments of wood, tail raised high in the air.

"You," the ogre growled, forgetting about Landry and Liliana as he turned to face the little cat.

The only sign that Ardus was nervous was the tiniest twitch at the end of his tail.

"Yes. Here I am." Ardus hopped over the last bit of wood and stood before the Ogre.

"And if you hurt my friends, you won't be getting what you want. So, I suggest you leave them alone." Ardus sat down and curled his tail around his feet.

The ogre's face purpled with rage.

"Fine. I'll leave them. For now. Now Where. Is. It," he growled.

"Hmm…" Ardus examined a paw. "I've heard so much about you, it's nice to finally see you in person. Is it true…everything they say about you?"

The ogre deflated, just a little, the purple turning to red. "What are people saying about me?" he asked, almost reluctantly.

"They're saying you're not only strong, you're the most powerful creature they've seen in over 200 years."

"They are?" an almost proud look gleamed from the beady eyes. "What else are they saying?"

"Hmmm…" Ardus arched his back and stretched. "That you have the ability to shapeshift. I didn't believe *that* of course. After all, everyone knows that's a myth." He yawned.

"But I can shapeshift," the ogre insisted.

"Can you now?" Ardus began to clean his whiskers. "Of course, that's an easy thing to *say*. I'll only believe it when I see it though."

"I can." The purple began to seep back into the ogre's face. "Come on, ask me. I'll change into anything you want."

Ardus continued to clean his whiskers. "I suppose this could be amusing. Let me think….could you change into a lion?"

The ogre closed his eyes and instantly, a lion replaced him.

Liliana clutched Landry's hand tightly, wondering what Ardus was doing. It would be no use to escape the ogre only to be replaced by something equally dangerous. The lion was huge, all sharp teeth and claws. It shook its mane, and began to pace the room, before lifted its head and roared the sound reverberating through the room until the floor trembled under the force of it. Ardus jumped back, all the hair on his back standing straight up.

Then, just as quickly as it appeared, it disappeared, and the ogre was back, looking none the worse for wear.

"See. It's true," pride laced the ogre's voice.

"I suppose." Ardus regained his composure. "But then again, you were changing into something the same *size* as you. That's probably the easier way to shapeshift."

The ogre began to look upset. "What? Is that not good enough for you?"

"No, no, if that's what you can do, it's very.....nice. But I've heard of shapeshifters, and not so long ago either....that can shift into something much smaller than the size they are. But maybe you aren't able to do that."

"How small?" the ogre growled.

"No, no. I wouldn't want you to fail." Ardus golden eyes gleamed.

"How. Small," the ogre insisted.

"Well..." Ardus cocked his head to the side. "Maybe as small as a...mouse."

Instantly, the ogre disappeared. There, on the floor, was a mouse—a tiny brown mouse, with bright black eyes and a long pink tail. Snap. Ardus pounced. He grabbed the mouse and gave it one vigorous shake.

"There." Ardus stepped away from the mouse, now laying in a crumpled heap on the floor. "That's better." He spit a hair out of his mouth. "Well? Are you just going to sit there staring? We have lots of things to do." Ardus put his tail in the air proudly and stalked toward the door.

"But—that's it?" Liliana was stunned.

"No, we still have plenty of other things to do. But the ogre is taken care of if that's what you mean. Although I'm going to need a drink, that tasted awful,"Ardus complained as he stepped toward the door.

"Oh." Liliana followed Ardus silently down the stairs.

"First, we're going to have to get some people in here. It's been left for a while, and there's so much to do." Ardus sniffed, as they emerged from the carriage house into the bright sunlight.

"Ardus, what just happened?" Liliana stopped outside the carriage house.

"Fine. I'll explain everything. But first let's go inside. I really do need a drink." Ardus led the way through the overgrown kitchen garden to a back entrance. They entered into the kitchen, where Liliana pumped some water into a bowl and set it down. Ardus lapped at the water before hopping up on the table and curling his tail.

"The ogre needed me because I'm the keeper of the estate. No one can come or go without my say so. That's why he could only get as far as the carriage house."

"If you're the keeper of the estate, then why were you all the way in Lovan?" Liliana asked.

"Well, it's a long story, but the last Marquis of Carabas was the last in his line."

Here, Landry and Liliana exchanged looks, before she lowered her lashes in shame. "I knew it. But I also knew you probably had your reasons," Landry admitted.

Liliana threaded her fingers together on top of the table. "I'm sorry, I wanted to tell you. Did everyone know?" she was horrified at the thought of everyone giggling about it behind her back.

Landry shook his head. "I don't think so." He put his hand on hers. "It doesn't change anything you know."

"Ahem." Ardus cleared his throat pointedly, drawing their attention back to himself. "Anyways." He picked up where he had left off. "After the last Marquis, I was approached by queen Penelope. I was really no more than a kitten at the time. She flattered me, told me how amazing I was. Then, she asked me if she would be able to have the use of the estate to use as a hideaway. When life at court became too much, she would escape to here. That sort of thing. I was so pleased and proud to be noticed by her, that of course I agreed. Foolishly, as I was later to find out, she did want it as a hideaway, but only because she didn't want people to know what she was up to." Ardus twitched his tail.

"What was she up to?" Liliana burned with curiosity.

"Dark magic. And she used it to find all sorts of artifacts to make herself more powerful. But she kept this all hidden from me. I should have known; the signs were there. But I suppose I chose not to see them."

"How did you find out what she was doing then?"

"I saw her one day, in the audience room; she had the mirror with her. I'd seen her use it often enough. But I never really paid much attention to what she was doing with it. It just seemed like another toy. But this time was different. She was staring into it as if she was possessed. And then, someone came out of it. Two people actually."

"Was that?"

"Prince Frederich and Princess Lucie. Yes." Ardus finished the sentence Landry was about to ask. "I was hiding; no one knew I was even there, and I watched as there was a big fight. It was clear she intended to harm them at the least, kill them at the most. And it was then I knew, she was evil."

"So then what happened?"

"Then she left, and only came back after Lucie and Frederich were already away."

"That's when things got really bad; she wandered the halls until all hours of the night, muttering to herself, plotting, and planning. Then, one day she disappeared, flew into the sky and I never saw her again."

"That must have been when she attacked Lucie."

"I thought I would be left in peace. The staff came back, and everything was getting back to normal. But then, the ogre came. Of course, I didn't know it was an ogre. I thought it was just a girl. She said her name was Cherry. She actually seemed quite helpless, sweet really."

"Cherry?" Landry narrowed his eyes. "I know that name well. She's the shapeshifter who took Celine's place."

"Yes, Cherry was quite the mischievous one. She had me fooled for a while. I took her in, thinking she could work in the kitchens. But it wasn't too long until she had the run of the place. She talked the housekeeper into letting her clean, and got into all the rooms, searching, always searching."

"Do you know what she was looking for?" Landry asked.

"Anything she could use to get stronger, and her ultimate goal was to become the next Marquis. So in truth, she wanted everything." Ardus twitched his tail with annoyance.

"Can there even be another Marquis of Carabas; I thought you said the line died out.

"*That* line died out, the title still stands," the little cat answered. "As the keeper of the title, I can choose a new line if I wish."

Landry nodded, as Liliana gave him a questioning look. "I've heard of this before. I didn't know it still happened though."

"Are you saying, Cherry, or the ogre rather, tried to force you to give her the title."

Ardus bristled. "As if anyone could force *me*. But I knew I couldn't stay either, so I waited until she was away one day, and left. But not before I made sure she wouldn't be able to come into the property. I set up protection around it, that's why she had to stay in the carriage house. It was a long journey, and I was very, very tired when I reached Annecy. It was only your kindness that saved me."

"My kindness?" Liliana raised her head.

"Yes, you rescued me from a dog, then you left out food for me, you brought me into your house when it was cold, and you shared your affection with me." Ardus rubbed his head against her arm. "That was when I decided." He stopped to clean his whiskers.

CHAPTER 26

"Decided what?" Landry and Liliana spoke in unison.

"Decided that you would be the new line of Carabas."

"I can't be a Marquis!" Liliana exclaimed.

"Of course, you can." Ardus purred. "In fact, since Landry is here, we can make it happen right now." He stood up and trotted to the kitchen door. "Follow me," he said over his shoulder.

Liliana and Landry followed Ardus down a long narrow hallway to a large study on the main floor. Ardus nudged the door open and stepped inside.

"All you have to do, is put your name in the ledger. Since Landry is a member of the royal family, he can sign it and make it official. He looked at Landry who nodded in agreement.

Liliana's head whirled with what seemed like a wild plan. "Are you sure about this?" she asked Ardus.

"I've never been surer in my life. Why, don't you want to be the Marquis?" Ardus sounded put out.

"It's such a big responsibility. I don't know if I can take care of all those people," Liliana admitted.

"You've already done it," Ardus insisted. "Who was it who made sure people were fed when the ogre destroyed the village? Who was it who allowed the people from the mining camp to go hunting, and who was it who came here at my suggestion even though you were risking your life? You are the most qualified person I can think of for this position."

Liliana sat at the wide mahogany desk, "If it doesn't work out, will I be able to reconsider?"

"I suppose if we must." Ardus scampered across a stack of books and poked his paw at a wide leather volume. Landry opened the volume, paging through until he came to the last page of writing.

"Here," Ardus laid his paw on the space.

Hand trembling with nerves, Liliana wrote her name into the space Ardus was pointing at. "And now you."

Landry took the quill and scrawled his initials.

"There. It's settled. You're the official Marquis of Carabas. See, you were telling the truth all along," Ardus' voice held a note of triumph.

A sense of relief washed over Liliana. She turned to Landry. "I know I might be the Marquis *now*. But I'm sorry I misled you; I hated every minute of it, and I promise never to do it again. She winced at the residual hurt lurking in the green eyes.

"All right. All right," Ardus interrupted their conversation. "Now that's taken care of, we have a lot of things to do."

"Where do we start?" Liliana realized she knew nothing about running an estate; it couldn't be that different from her Father's business, she thought to herself.

"First, we need to get some staff. Then, we're going to have a ball."

"A ball?" It was the last thing Liliana expected the reclusive cat to say.

"Yes, a ball will cement your position and introduce you to your people. I think three weeks should be enough time to get ready."

Liliana glanced at Landry, who had a spark in his eye. "A ball sounds perfect."

The next few hours were a flurry of activity. The staff, terrified, after first being bullied by Penelope, then threatened by the ogre, were hiding in nearby villages where they had taken refuge. Landry was sent to retrieve them, carrying an official proclamation dictated by the cat himself.

Within the next few days, the castle became a hive of activity as people trickled in from all directions. Soon, the kitchens were up and running, food was being delivered and stockpiled, and staterooms prepared.

Liliana was in the pasture when the king arrived. Thankfully, some kind person had let the horses out to graze, and they had gone a bit feral from lack of human contact. Liliana was coaxing a small brown mare into being put in a harness when she heard the clatter of many hoofbeats coming up the lane. The mare shied away, frightened at the sudden noise and activity. Giving up on the mare, Liliana ran to meet them.

"Landry told us everything!" Celine exclaimed, greeting her new friend. "I can't believe the ogre is actually gone; Ardus is a genius." She jumped off her horse, giving Liliana a squeeze. Liliana squeezed her back as the two girls walked arm in arm toward the castle.

Celine insisted on getting a tour of the castle immediately, taking particular interest in the audience hall, the scene of the epic battle between her sister-in-law and Penelope.

"I didn't realize it would be so big." Celine sat on the steps of the dais. The room was no longer dusty. Instead, it smelled of the lemon soap that had been used to clean the floors. Everything was beginning to shine and sparkle, the staff so delighted to be returned to their home and have a new mistress that they put in extra effort to make everything perfect.

"Celine. There is something I have to tell you. Something important." Liliana's swallowed hard.

"What is it Liliana?" Celine turned her cornflower blue eyes to her friend.

"I'll understand if you don't feel the same way about me after you hear this. But I don't want there to be anything between us. I haven't been completely honest with you." Liliana lowered her lashes, starting at the pattern in the marble floor.

Celine furrowed her brow, waiting for Liliana to continue.

"The truth is, I wasn't the Marquis of Carabas when I met you. I was only a regular girl from a village in Lovan. The cat asked me to play the part, and I agreed. I hated lying to you, and I'm so sorry. I'll understand if you don't want to be my friend anymore, but I hope you can find it in your heart to forgive me." She turned her eyes to Celine, chewing her lip.

"I appreciate you telling me this." Celine frowned, thinking for a moment. "I know you had your reasons. I did suspect, and so did Landry and Alex. But we know you. You're kind and good inside and it shows in everything you do— how you take care of people and make them your own. That's your truth. You're going to be the best Marquis this estate has ever seen; I just know it." Celine gave Liliana's arm a squeeze.

"Do you really think so?" the tension seeped away as the huge weight lifted from Liliana's shoulders.

"Definitely. And the prettiest too." Celine winked. "Speaking of pretty, don't we have a ball to get ready for? You're going to need a pretty dress. I found some bolts of fabric when I was poking around earlier, and I found something you're going to love."

CHAPTER 27

Liliana twisted and turned in front of the mirror. The silk fabric Celine suggested was something she would never usually consider. The deep red was so bold, but Celine had insisted. Folds of soft red floated around her. In her hair was a band of embroidered ribbon Sokdi had given her earlier, colourful flowers in the traditional pattern. Liliana loved having her friendship with the Antarai on display. Grateful for their help, Liliana hoped to start a long and fruitful alliance with the proud people.

She smoothed her dress, stepping into the corridor.

The ballroom was stunning, masses of candles and fresh flowers decorating the space with colour and light. Ardus sat proudly in his place of honour, on a tasselled cushion, where he observed the proceedings, green eyes glinting. He purred as Liliana stroked his head, scanning the celebrating throngs.

Across the room, Liliana's eyes met and held a different pair of green eyes. Landry. He abruptly left his father's side, eyes glued to Liliana.

"You look.... beautiful." He swallowed hard as he closed Liliana's hand in his. Suddenly shy, she lowered her gaze, heart beating fast and loud in her chest.

"Would you like to dance?" Landry cleared his throat, gesturing toward the dance floor. The Antarai had offered their services; a collection of instruments were playing a merry tune. Liliana nodded, allowing herself to be pulled into the dance. When the music stopped, they were near the French doors leading to the garden. Without a word, Landry took her hand and led her down the path.

Liliana let the cool breeze cool her hot cheeks as she breathed in the scent of freshly cut grass and pine.

"I know it's selfish, but I just wanted you to myself for a minute. It's been so busy the last three weeks." Landry leaned against the balustrade.

"I know, I still can't believe all this is happening," Liliana admitted.

"We're leaving next week. Father wants Celine to continue the tour," Landry abruptly changed the subject.

Liliana went cold. She knew Landry would leave sometime, but running the vast the estate alone terrified her. Where would she even start? She tilted her head, waiting for Landry to continue.

He cleared his throat. "I was wondering, that is.... if you want.... I could."

Liliana held her breath.

"I could stay and help with the estate. Father taught me everything about ours. And..." Landry paused. "I want to spend time with you."

"You do?" the tension eased, as a spark of hope lit inside her chest.

"I do. A lot more time. Forever, if you'll have me." For the first time, Landry's eyes were uncertain.

"Yes." Liliana turned and threw her arms around his neck. "Yes, I want you to stay."

He held her close, his arms warm around her, and Liliana laid her head on his chest.

"This is where you two sneaked off to. Father's about to make a speech—we've been searching everywhere for you." Celine and Alex burst into their bubble.

"Wait a minute." Celine peered into their faces. "Am I interrupting something."

"No." Liliana blushed.

"Yes," Landry insisted.

"I wondered how long it was going to take you," Alex teased his brother.

Hand warm against the small of her back, Landry guided Liliana inside to join the party.

THE END.

Curious about that abandoned house in the forest? Find out what happens next by reading book four in the Crown and the Sceptre Series- LOYAL – A Retelling of Red Riding Hood.

Don't miss out!

Visit the website below and you can sign up to receive emails whenever Kristina J Jordan publishes a new book. There's no charge and no obligation.

https://books2read.com/r/B-A-KPEO-USDRB

BOOKS 2 READ

Connecting independent readers to independent writers.

Also by Kristina J Jordan

The Crown and the Sceptre
Free A Fairy Tale Retelling of Rapunzel
Strong - A Fairy Tale Retelling of the Princess and the Pea
True A Fairy Tale Retelling of Puss in Boots
Pretty - A fairy Tale Retelling of the Frog Prince
Loyal - A Fairy Tale Retelling of Red Riding Hood